MW00441855

In loving memory of Ms. Mary Jane Jones. Thank you for always encouraging me to let the world see my light.

Printed in the United States of America
First Printing, 2020
ISBN 9781087932255
Mae AH Productions, LLC
Charlotte, NC 28262
www.angelaleshawn.com

Acknowledgements

Just like any speech, I have to thank God first. It is because of his grace that I have been able to complete a story from beginning to end. With him, all things have been made possible.

To my best friends, who believed before I wrote a word on any page. They don't like attention, so I won't put their names here. :-) I couldn't have completed Love Notes without your encouragement. I wouldn't have had the courage to be an author without your extra push. No matter what successes God blesses me with, our bond will be one of my greatest gifts.

To my crew, I could write a whole other book about how much you've supported me over the years. If I wanted to sell potatoes on the side of the road, you all would ask which road we were going to. Many of you have been riding with me since high school; others a little less. It is not lost on me how lucky I am.

To my parents & Godparents, who always encouraged me to be whatever I wanted to be. Those titles have changed many times over the years. You never questioned, or waivered, you only believed. Thank you is never enough, but **THANK YOU.**

To my sisters, who I love beyond measure. Thank you for always keeping it real with me. If it was good, you told me. If it wasn't, you told me that too. When I doubted (which was every step of the way) you reminded me that I was more than a conqueror.

To each person who read a chapter of this book in its early stages, thank you. To each person who respected my absence while I completed this book, thank you. To every person who bought this book without having an idea what it was about, thank you.

Lastly, to Amirah Cook. You shared your wisdom with me and created a safe space for me to create. When I believed I was less than, you changed my perspective. Love Notes was created because of the tools you gave me. In the words of Tyler Perry, you never know whose dreams are attached to yours.

Author Bio

Angela Leshawn is a lover of words. It can be Hip-hop, R&B, or a good book. Every story deserves to be told. Originally from Syracuse NY, she currently resides in Charlotte NC. A number cruncher by day (Accountant) and storyteller by night. Her superpower is being able to bring anyone into whatever world she's created in her head. She is inspired by her favorite scripture Isaiah 43:19.

Chapter 1

"I KNOW THAT GOD HAS A PLAN, BUT THIS ONE IS REALLY HARD TO ACCEPT."
– Harper Stewart, *The Best Man Holiday*

The dark has always been my place of solace. Choosing a profession where people die, you'd expect to be used to it when people - you know - die. Five years as an ER nurse, and I wasn't. I'd never been. So, I found my solace in the dark. When one of my patients died, I mourned for them. Always in the dark. Always with my special candle.

"Ada, somebody die again?"

His deep voice both startled and comforted me. My husband of five years towered in the doorway of our front room. At 6'4, he looked more like a secret agent than a classical piano teacher. I never knew how long he'd been watching until he made it known. The flicker of the candle showed his smooth brown skin and glimpses of his full beard. He rubbed his fingers through it while waiting for the answer he knew I'd give

With tear-filled eyes, I replied, "yes.

With two steps forward, he was standing over me. He crouched down to my level. Staring in my eyes with concern, he asked

"You want me to sit with you?"

I shook my head.

"You sure?"

Whatever look I gave him was enough assurance because he gently cupped my chin. Three kisses followed. Forehead. Cheek. Lips. Three was our number of completion. None of our kisses were complete unless there were three.

"Change out of your scrubs and meet me in the spot." He had given an order and not a request.

Before I could rise from my seat on the floor, the soft sweet sounds of jazz flowed through the house. Amare was starting a ritual of his own. I grabbed the stack of yellow sticky notes beside me and wrote "Abagail Moore" in big, bold letters. She'd lost her battle with a brain aneurysm in my ER today. I placed the corner of the note in the burning candle.

Ashes to ashes. Dust to dust. I spoke in a whisper, and before the flame could consume the note entirely, I placed it in the trash bin by the door.

In my life, I learned early that the only thing I could do right is help people. Cooking, meh. Cleaning, nah. I am almost always in jeans and a t-shirt. My hair is either in a bun or ponytail.

There's nothing about my pear shape and low eyes that stuck out in a crowd. All the things that society valued women on, I was in short supply. But if you need me, I'm there. If you're sick, I'll nurse you to health. If I don't know the answers to your problem, I will help you find it.

My grandmother would always say, 'Girl! Good thing God sends help and not company. 'Cause you gonna need a whole lot of help" This would usually come after I'd just burned another pot of grits or while she was rewashing a dish I'd supposedly just finished cleaning.

I couldn't help but stop and think about the day God sent my husband. I wish I knew then that I'd be the help. It probably would have made our first interaction a little less tense.

***

"Ada, Room 1304. Stab wound victim."

I was sixteen hours into a twelve-hour shift. The last thing I wanted was yet another patient. Lorie, my mentor at the time, sensed my reluctance to take the chart and tried to sweeten the pot

"It's only eight stitches, and I promise you can go home right after."

Hill Medical Center was planted in one of the most underserved neighborhoods in Chicago. We regularly got gunshot and stab wound victims. We rarely got the funding we needed to take care of those who couldn't afford medical care. Which means we were always short-staffed. My friends repeatedly asked me why with a doctorate in Nurse Practice, did I choose this place. I could be making double the money with fewer hours at one of the fancier clinics. My answer was always simple, "this is where I am most needed.

"Give me the chart," I sighed

Room 1304 sat at the end of the hall; it was one of the ICU's smallest rooms. We all hated this room because you'd be on top of your patient to get anything done. I'm sure every bit of the aggravation from the day was apparent in my voice when I spoke.

"Amare Wilson. Can you tell me about your injury?" My eyes never left the chart

"Somebody stabbed me."

I think it was always his voice that got me first. It sounded like warm honey. Soothing yet strong.

"Are you gonna stitch me up? I need to get back to my students."

I didn't realize it, but I'd been staring at him since he first spoke. Brown skin, full lips, and dark brown eyes stared right back at me.

"Ummm...Yes, I just need to get more information. How were you injured?" I asked as I sat on the small stool next to the exam table.

"A fight broke out at my school. I tried to break it up, and a young boy pulled a knife."

"Would you like to file a police report?" I asked.

"And put one of my own in the system, I'll pass."

"It's the procedure that we ask. I'll notate the chart." I made sure my response was just as short as he had been.

"Any allergies?

"Only to wasted time," He said with an eye roll.

At this point, I was over his attitude. He was visibly irritated, and I was equally tired. "You're the one who needs stitches, sir. I could be home" The conversation in my head went different than the words I spoke aloud.

"I'm just going to step out of the room, Mr. Wilson. I'll just need you to take your shirt off and put on the gown behind you. Leave the right side open. I'll stitch you up, and you can be on your way."

"Good and call me Amare," He said as he started to tug on the blood-stained white V-neck t-shirt he wore.

"Oh, now you want to be friendly." I thought.

As I turned to exit the room, his voice once again stopped me.

"You don't have to leave; I don't mind undressing with you in here."

I turned my back anyway.

"I'm all done." He said shortly after that.

When I turned around, he had opted only to take his shirt off and drape the gown over the shoulder that had not been wounded. Sensing my annoyance, he explained.

"I just need this to go as quickly as possible. I mentor one of the boys in the fight, and I need to get back to him."

No response from me. Instead, I handed Amare my suture kit and instructed him to sit very still. I stitched him up in complete silence, with only occasional winches on his part. The room was so small, and I had to position myself in the corner behind his right shoulder to get each stitch in. Every time I needed more thread, my body would press against his slightly.

It didn't seem to affect him as much as it did me, though. His first words came after I'd completed the last stitch.

"Wow. That was quick. I can barely see a scar."

I nodded.

"Your parents must be proud. You don't see many black women in this field."

Instead of saying thanks or nothing at all, I said:

"They're dead."

To my surprise, he replied.

"Mine too. Home invasion. You?"

"Mother, cancer when I was six. Father had a stroke in my senior year of college."

"Damn. Sorry to hear that." He said while finally getting both arms through his shirt.

"Me too."

And with that, he was gone. I signed my name on the bottom of his chart and headed home. In my mind, he was just another patient, but two weeks later, I received two dozen roses. The card read:

"I feel like I owe you. I just can't decide if it's for being an asshole or you putting me back together. Maybe you can help me decide over dinner?"

***

The overwhelming smell of lavender brought me to the present. The scent led me to the bathroom, where Amare was already submerged in the water. While we were apart, he'd lit small candles and placed them around our clawfoot tub. Now it was my turn to stare.

"What you waitin' for, strip!" He said with a smirk.

We kept a bin in the hallway labeled contaminated, and that is where I threw my scrubs before I slid my body between his legs. Our tub barely held the both of us, but I didn't care because being skin to skin with him always relaxed me.

"Don't worry. You always feel better after our date day. You have to make it through one more shift, babe." He whispered that after we'd sat in silence for a few minutes. My response was not audible, just an exhausted exhale

"If that doesn't make you feel better, you can always turn around and sit on my lap." He said, giving each one of my shoulders a kiss.

"Or – and just hear me out – I can turn around and sit on your shoulders," I said with a smirk.

"I think I have one more kiss left in me. Come on."

My final shift of the week always dragged, but I had a feeling it was about to get better as I headed back to the nursing station.

"Aww, Lauren. You got flowers?" I yelled down the hall.

She was holding a bouquet of lavender roses, smelling and touching each one. Lauren graduated nursing school only a year ago, and I'd been training her from the moment she'd entered the doors of Hill Memorial. She was the perfect balance of sassy and smart.

"Now, bitch... you know these aren't for me!" She hissed as I had gotten closer. I took the flowers and began searching for a card.

"Ada, we are getting sick of you acting surprised every time these flowers come here. Your husband sends you flowers every week." The other nurses joined around as she laughed.

I was the only nurse on the shift who was married. Every week I endured the same playful banter, and every week I rolled my eyes while isolating my middle finger towards them. Lauren took the card before I could read it.

"Shit, I wish I liked someone enough to tell them my real name, let alone where I worked."

The card told me where to meet Amare later this evening.

"Are you ready for rounds, or are we going to act surprised that there is a card?"

I let my middle finger express my feelings for Lauren's comment.

Our afternoon rounds started with Mr. Jason. A 60-year-old black man who had been admitted for complications with pneumonia. His wife had found him passed out in their home before calling 911. She'd been by his side every day since, and today, we'd come to bring them the good news.

"Hi, Mr. Jason." I said as I entered the room. I passed his chart over to Lauren and let her take the lead. While she checked his vitals, I pulled out my phone to text Amare.

Got the flowers. Love them as always. Can't wait to see you later.

I ended it with a kiss emoji, just in time for Lauren to finish up with our patient.

"You will be discharged today, Mr. Jason."

The room was silent. Mr. Jason and his wife looked at each other like we'd just told them their dog died. Not the expression we had hoped from someone who had been revived only two days before.

"Did you hear her, Mr. Jason? You're going home." I said.

And then, the tears. First, the wife and then himself. The tears were followed by thank you's, and before we knew it, we all were crying. Our joy was short-lived because immediately after I released Mr. Jason from a bear hug, my hospital phone buzzed

Mass casualties. All hands-on deck.

Without thinking, I began running towards the triage area, while Lauren ran towards our nurses' station to get an update. I grabbed the first gurney I saw and started frantically searching for a chart.

"What's going on?" I asked a tall, green-eyed doctor running by.

He managed to stop long enough to tell me that there had been a mass shooting. A gunman opened fire on a gathering, and these people were just in the wrong place at the wrong time.

"ADA!" Lauren appeared behind me with her scrubs covered in blood.

"You're needed in room 1304."

The look in her eyes told me that there was something more, but she didn't speak it. She just ran and motioned for me to follow behind. When we arrived at room 1304, she stopped and blocked the door.

"What is it?!" I said. "Who is it? One of ours?" At this point, I was rambling.

"Ada," it was his voice that got me. The voice that had been soothing my worries and cares over the last five years now sounded weak. I pushed past Lauren with a vengeance to find my husband laid on a gurney. Bandages covered the gunshot wound on his chest as doctors tried to stop the bleeding.

Words escaped me. I had to be dreaming. This could not be what my eyes were seeing. I don't know how long I stood there before I spoke, nor do I know what I said. The doctors explained that Amare tried to help, and the gunman turned and opened fire on him. He'd been shot in the chest and lost an incredible amount of blood.

"We've stopped the bleeding, but he needs surgery. He wouldn't let us take him before seeing you."

I shook my head and walked past Dr. Davis to the side of Amare's hospital bed. I hoisted myself up to lay beside him. By this time, Amare had gone unconscious. I had lost the ability to speak, but my hand traced his face hoping he would wake. That never happened.

There was no more time left, and as they wheeled Amare out of Room 1304, I knew that would be the last time I would see him. Two hours later, my worst fear was confirmed. My husband had succumbed to his injuries during surgery.

That night Lauren drove me home, and after an hour of convincing her I'd be fine, she left. Out of habit, I dragged myself into the front room. The smell of his cologne still lingered, and that was enough to open the flood gates. I lay on the floor sobbing and gasping for air until there was nothing left.

Finding my strength, I stood to my feet. The stack of yellow notes was still sitting on the mantle where I'd left them the night before. I lit my candle. Trembling, I wrote, "My Heart" in big, bold letters. Then allowed the flame to devour it.

"YOU SHO IS UGLY."

- Suge Avery, The Color Purple

Warm. My body was too damn warm. The type of warmth that could only come from another body ignorantly laying on top of you. My brother Windell is by far the most annoying person you will ever meet. When we were kids, he would always wake me up by laying his entire body on top of mine. You would think in his older age; those childish things would be put away. But no, they were not.

"Windell, please let me sleep." I murmured from underneath his body weight

"Nope, you have to get up, Ada. We need to talk!"

Talking, eating, or doing anything outside of sleeping had not interested me in the last year. I knew Windell was not going to let up, so I used all my might to push him off and sat on the edge of the couch.

"Look at you." He said softly.

My hair was in a matted bun on top of my head. I couldn't tell you the last time I washed it. I had on dirty black sweats and a matching hoodie designed with specks of whatever food I forced myself to eat that week. My usual athletic frame was skin and bones. He didn't have to tell me. I knew what I looked like, death.

"You have been living here for a year. You have no job, and based on the stack of red envelopes laying on my counter, you're out of money." He continued.

There's never any privacy with siblings, especially when you're living under their roof. Windell is a very matter-of-fact person. He was never one to hold his tongue. It did not matter if you were family, friend, or foe. If Windell had an issue, he would bring it straight to you. He towered over me at six feet and was very much into his appearance. Even today, as he gave me a look of pity, he did it while dressed in Burberry loungewear.

I gave a deep sigh.

"What do you want me to do? I told you I couldn't go back into the medical field."

After Amare passed, I said I would give myself two weeks before going back to Hill Memorial in Chicago. Two weeks turned into four, which then turned into six. Pretty soon, my bills motivated me to step back in the door. I had hoped helping people heal their wounds would help me heal my own. The first day in the hospital started a normal one.

I'd even gotten to work early. As soon as the automatic doors opened, my breath shortened. I felt my chest getting tight, and before I knew it, I collapsed. Though they assured me my panic attack was normal for grieving people, I took that as a sign to sell my home and move to Atlanta with Windell. His loft apartment had a spare bedroom, but I opted for the couch most nights. Staying here was supposed to be temporary, but a year had flown by in a flash.

"I wasn't thinking about the medical field. We wouldn't want a repeat of last year." Windell said, bringing my attention back to him.

"Well, what were you thinking? I said, eyeing him suspiciously.

Windell pressed his hands together and slightly turned his body towards me.

"I was thinking of something more entry-level." He started.

"I have a friend named Addison. She is the executive assistant for Eko. Before you ask, He is an R&B singer. He is getting ready to head out on a sold-out summer tour, and they are looking for another assistant. I told her you'd be great for it."

I opened my mouth to interject, but he cut me off.

"Your interview is tomorrow."

His eyes told me I didn't have any choice in the matter. Though I hated to admit it, he was right. Amare's life insurance had covered the funeral expenses. The money I received from our house's sale covered his medical expenses, what was left after that Sallie Mae came looking for. I took the remaining of our savings to move to Atlanta and decided to play "Catch me if you can" with the rest of my debt.

The last time I mustered up the nerve to check my bank account, it had less than $100. How long could I expect Windell to take care of me?

"I'll go," I said half-heartedly.

"Oh, I know you're going." He said with a laugh.

"I feel bad for you, but tears don't pay the bills, sis."

I showed him my favorite finger. The same one I would flash at the nurses' station.

"Can I go back to sleep now?" I whined.

"Sleep? No, but what you can do is shower that smell off you." He said in disgust

For the first time in what seemed like forever, I laughed

That night Windell took me shopping at Neiman's for an outfit to wear to the interview the next day. He told me I needed to impress Addison, so he made sure that my dress was Diane Von Furstenberg. When the total came to over $500, I stopped him.

"This is too much, Windell. I do not care how much money you make in data protection."

"Consider it an investment. You will pay me back."

He emphasized the "will" a little too much for my liking, but beggars can't be choosers.

Afterward, we went back home for my crash course in the music industry. I learned that the tour's first leg would hit six cities and then the second leg another six. Eko did a mix of singing and rapping. His new single was already platinum, and his self-titled album had been number one on the charts for the last four weeks. His music videos showed me everything I needed to know about him.

He had no less than six chains wrapped around his neck, a watch for each arm, and shirts did not exist in his world. His Instagram showed him at every party with a different girl and stacks of cash. How Windell thought I would be a good fit as his assistant was beyond me. I went to sleep, hoping for my own sake, he was right.

Located in Brighton Park, Dance 101 was a dance studio every known celebrity used. Atlanta traffic caused the twenty-minute drive to take me over an hour. I managed to get to the front door just before Addison locked it. Normally open to all dance levels, today Dance 101 was closed for

Eko's personal use.

"Diane Von Furstenberg?" Addison asked, blocking the entrance

Grateful that Windell had shown me her Instagram the night before, I extended my right hand towards her.

"Hi, my name is Ada. I'm here for the interview."

She looked at my hand and then up at me before repeating her words

"Diane Von Furstenberg?"

"Ummmm, yes." I said, looking down at my black and yellow A-line dress.

"Good choice. Follow me." She said, turning on her six-inch heels and finally letting me in.

Addison was really, really...white. She walked with a purpose that was paid for many generations ago. With tanned skin, her long blonde hair stopped just above her ass, and she was wearing designer from head to toe. I briefly wondered how she afforded the diamond Tiffany bracelets she wore on each wrist. As we passed dark empty rooms, she began to rattle off information about the position.

"What I need is someone to help with the dancers. These people can't even make it anywhere on time." She said, waving her arm toward the studio on the right. Inside I saw four dancers stretching and a five-person band setting up behind them. She ushered me into the studio just across the hall.

"So, the position isn't an assistant for Eko?" I asked once we were inside.

"I am Eko's only assistant. You would be the assistant to the assistant." She made sure to stress the last part as she took a seat in one of the two chairs placed in the middle of the floor.

I shook my head in agreeance and sat across from her.

"This isn't really an interview. Your brother has done some tech work for us. So, if he says you're a good fit, I trust it. Here."

Addison handed me a piece of paper with the title "Rules" on it.

"Read through this, and when I come back, we can discuss." I had no time to ask any questions before she was out the door. I closed the notebook I brought and began to read.

Rules:
1. You must ALWAYS wear ALL BLACK.
2. Never speak directly to Eko or look him directly in the eye.
3. You must stay between 120-135 pounds. Any weight gain will result in immediate termination.
4. You are on call 24/7. A missed call or text will result in immediate termination.
5. You cannot eat any beef or pork.
6. Your hair and nails must always be presentable. Chipped polish or unfavorable hairstyles will result in immediate termination.

"Unfavorable hairstyles?!? No hamburgers. No bacon. Is this a TikTok skit?" I said aloud to the walls of the empty room. Who would want to do this? Windell had lost his mind. I pulled out my phone to text him just how much.

> Is this a joke? They are nuts! I passed a Target on the way here. A red shirt and Khakis wouldn't be so bad!

Before I could hit send, Addison returned and sat in a chair directly across from me.

"So, Ada. What do you think?" She said in her perky voice.

"I think I've wasted your time." I began. "I'm not sure if Windell told you, but I have a doctorate. It seems like this position wouldn't fit my skill set. Thank you for meeting with me, though." I gave a fake smile, and with that, it was my turn to get up and leave.

"You didn't waste my time! I hope your skill set finds something else that pays $2,500 a week." She called after me.

My pride told me to keep walking, but my bills pushed me to speak.

"I'm sorry, did you say $2,500 a week?"

"I did. Cash." She said with a smirk.

I laughed and said, "Well, maybe, I think six cities won't be so bad."

"Unfortunately, that isn't my decision. It will be Eko's. "

"Okay, where is he?"

"You'll get a text for the next steps in the interview process. Just stay ready. Do you remember how to get out?"

I shook my head and proceeded towards the exit. That night at Windell's, I made sure the volume on my phone was at the max. I checked my notifications every five minutes. Once the clock read two am, I gave up. Sometime after I dozed off, my phone shined bright.

Magic City. Tomorrow. 11 pm. Ask for Bug.

Chapter 3

"IT'S GOING TO BE A HOASIS TONIGHT!"
- Quentin, The Best Man

Magic City Strip Club was one of the most popular strip clubs in Atlanta. If you didn't know it, you'd be able to tell once you got within a two-mile radius of the building. After sitting in standstill traffic for what seemed like hours, I opted to get out of my Lyft and walk the rest of the distance. I could hear the DJ from a block away, and as I got closer, I was met by a line wrapped around the corner. Addison had sent a second text message telling me to go straight to the front door and ask for someone named Bug.

"Back of the line," The security guard barked as I walked to the front door.

"I-I'm here for Bug," I stuttered.

He stood no more than 5'6, but you can tell he compensated for his lack of height by regularly lifting weights in the gym. My eyes darted to his right hip, and I saw that he was licensed to carry. I immediately regretted not making Windell come with me to this "second interview."

"Bug, you said?" he was yelling over the commotion outside.

"Yes, my name is Ada."

He motioned for me to stand to the side and disappeared into the building. When he returned, a tall figure was following close behind.

"Are you Ada?" The tall figure asked.

"Yes." I answered.

"I'm Bug. Step inside for me." I walked in and stood directly to the right.

Magic City was overwhelming. So many things were going on at one time. There were two hundred and fifty people in a space that was built to hold half that. A small black stage with three poles was placed to see the show no matter where you were. Each pole had a different shade of brown girl.

One hanging upside down, slowly easing her body to the floor. The next spinning her body around in circles, only using her calves' strength to hold her up. The last girl was simply in a full split twerking. Surrounding the stage were leather armchairs and small cocktail tables. Off to the side were the VIP sections.

Each one was roped off with its own security. I could tell that these were reserved for the high rollers by the leather couches and private wait staff.

"Ada," Bug pulled me out of my trance.

"I need to pat you down."

"Okay," I said distractedly. I had become intrigued by one of the strippers who was now twerking in a full handstand.

"Arms out for me" Bug was now standing in front of me, blocking my view.

For the first time, I took a good look at the figure I had come to meet. He was tall. Real tall. At least six foot five. His skin was the smoothest of dark chocolate. Dressed in a black suit, with his hair cut low, he was all business.

"Now your purse." He said after finishing my pat-down.

I opened the small clutch I had brought, and he shined a small flashlight into it.

"That mace?" He asked.

"Ugh, yeah. I think my brother put that in there." I reached in and handed it over to him without question

"I'll give it back when you leave."

Satisfied with his search, he put the flashlight in his pocket with my mace.

"This should only take a second. When we get to the section, just stand off to the side. Eko has a weird way of vetting people, so do not take it personally if you don't make it past this point. Try not to look him in the eye. Follow me and stay close." He'd stepped closer so I could hear him over the loud music.

"$2,500 a week." I murmured

"What was that?" Bug said.

"Oh, nothing. Lead the way."

Staying close proved to be my first task of the night. The crowd seemed to split like Bug's red sea, but I had gotten lost twice in the ten steps we took. After the second time, Bug grabbed my wrist and dragged me the rest of the way. Eko's VIP section was not hard to miss. It took up the whole right side of the club. Two of the club's security guards blocked the entrance. They moved to the side when they saw Bug and I coming.

"You good?" He said as we got past the red ropes. I shook my head, removing my wrist from his grasp.

The inside of Eko's section could have been its own nightclub. If Uncle Luke had an offspring, Eko would be it. Six sets of tits - each a different shade - surrounded him on the leather couch he was standing on. It looked like Janet Jackson, and El Debarge had a love child. From his place on the sofa, I guessed he was medium height.

His skin was the color of butter pecan ice cream, and his hair was tapered on each side with long black curls falling from the middle. Three diamond chains were perched on his shirtless chest, and he was holding a fourth. When I asked Windell to describe Eko from the one time he met him, he gave me two words. Flashy Motherfucker. I had a front-row seat as to why.

Bug leaned into Eko's right ear and whispered something while pointing at me. Though I couldn't hear, I assumed he was introducing me, so I stepped forward and extended my right hand

"No. No. No. I don't know what kind of energy you carry; so, people don't touch me, and I don't touch them!" He yelled over the music. I took a step back and nearly tipped over a briefcase filled with diamond chains

"Sorry!" I said to the white man sitting on the other side of the table.

All Eko did was laugh.

"Sit right here." He said, instructing yellow tits to get up with a snap of a finger.

Taking my seat, I finally saw a familiar face. Addison had just arrived holding two glasses of champagne. She handed one to me, and I gratefully took it.

"Glad you made it." She said in a high-pitched squeaky voice. I had not heard this tone in the interview yesterday. I made a mental note of the faint white dust under her nostril as she sat on the other side of Eko.

"Twenty-five hundred dollars." I whispered into my glass of champagne. Out of the corner of my eye, I could see Eko still examining a diamond Cuban link chain.

"Ay Joe, how much is this?" he asked.

"About 30k." Joe responded.

"Hey, you! Bet you ain't never seen a motherfucker about to put thirty thousand dollars worth of diamonds around his neck, huh?"

At first, I didn't realize he was talking to me. I had been focusing on not drinking this champagne in one gulp while also trying not to look him in the eye. The chain landing in my lap grabbed my attention.

"Feel that new girl. Thirty thousand in diamonds. Bet you ain't felt no shit like that."

I picked up the Cuban without looking his way. The diamonds were beautiful, but the chain felt like a feather in my hands. I felt each diamond and then put one up to my mouth.

"Ay, hold up. What you doing?" Eko yelled, stepping down from the couch.

I ignored him and forced a big breath. The diamond fogged up immediately.

"It's fake," I yelled as I handed the chain back to him.

"What the fuck you mean it's fake?!" Eko looked from me to Joe.

"A real diamond doesn't fog up when you breathe on it. Condensation does not stick to real diamonds," I explained.

Joe stood up, preparing to plead his case.

"Who is this bitch? What does she know about diamonds?" His Italian accent was thick. Charging around the table, he stood in front of me. Out of nowhere, Bug appeared.

"What's going on over here?" He asked.

"Get this bitch out of the VIP!" Joe yelled.

The second bitch made me wish I had concealed that mace a little better. I nervously glanced at the rest of the club, thinking security must be making its way over. Everything was still business as usual around us.

"Just test the diamonds." I suggested.

"Yeah, let's just test the diamonds." Eko echoed.

Joe walked over to the briefcase, and hesitantly grabbed his diamond detector.

"Nah, let her do it." Eko said as he grabbed the detector and handed it to me.

Now I was nervous. What if I was wrong? It'd been a while since I'd done a diamond test, but it was practically in my DNA. I held the detector in my right hand and the Cuban in my left. I pressed the sensor to the diamond and waited. It was the longest thirty seconds of my life, but to my relief, nothing happened. There was no sound or light to indicate the necklace was real.

With a swift move, Eko jumped over me and grabbed Joe by the collar of his shirt.

"You think you can play me motherfucker?! Do you know who I am?"

I stood frozen.

"Get her out of here!" Eko gave direction to Bug without lifting a finger off Joe

The walk back to the entrance was a quick one. Bug had grabbed my wrist when we exited VIP, and I had no opportunity to get lost. When we made it outside of the front door, Bug offered to walk me to my car.

"I don't have one. I'll need to order my Lyft.

"Well, I'll stand out here with you."

To my surprise, the nearest driver was only five minutes away. I showed Bug my phone.

"It's five minutes from here. You don't have to wait."

His look told me that this wasn't an ask but a tell.

"How'd you know that diamond was fake?" He asked.

"My father was a jeweler, and so was his father before him. My brother and I worked in his shop until he died. I can spot a fake diamond from a mile away."

"Sorry to hear about your pops." He said just as my driver was pulling up.

To my surprise, Bug reached for my door, and I stepped inside.

"Thank you." I said, closing the door.

He walked away without another word. Before the driver could take off, I rolled down the window and yelled.

"Hey Bug!"

"Yeah?" he replied, turning around.

"My mace."

For the first time tonight, I saw the corners of his mouth turn up.

Windell was waiting for me when I got back to the apartment.

"How'd it go?"

I shrugged.

"I'm not sure." I said after a few seconds.

"Well, did you pass the second interview?" He probed

"I'm not sure." I repeated

I now realized that I had left the club without knowing if I had a job or not. Windell must have noticed the exhaustion in my face, so he didn't ask me any more questions.

"I'm going to get in the shower. Goodnight." I told him.

"A shower?!? Won't he do it!" Windell said with fake surprise

I showed him my favorite finger as I closed the door to the bathroom. Hot water was exactly what I needed to wash away tonight's disaster. Just before I could step inside, my phone vibrated with a text from Addison.

> You're in. Mercedes Benz Stadium. Tomorrow. 5pm.

Chapter 9

"IF I'M A BITCH, THEN YO MAMA'S A BITCH. BITCH!"
– Justice, Poetic Justice

A black town car was sent for me the day of the Atlanta show. Once inside, I found an envelope addressed to me. It was perched on top of an iPad, iPhone, and all-access backstage pass. There was a note attached that read:

Please sign and date the enclosed Non-Disclosure Agreement.
The contract inside was broken out into four sections:
  A.   Definition of confidential information
  B.   Exclusions of confidential information
  C.   Obligations
  D.   Time Period

After reading through each page twice, I realized this was just a legal way for them to tell me to keep my mouth shut. I was not allowed to take any pictures of or appear in any images with Eko. I had no intention of ever telling anyone's personal business, so I signed and placed the envelope in the one bag I could bring for the first six cities we visited.

The driver pulled up to the backstage entrance of Mercedes Benz Stadium. Tonight, Eko and his opener Eight would be performing for a sold-out crowd. I stepped out of the car to find Bug pacing back and forth. He looked relieved when he saw me coming.

"Addison told me to meet you. He said, sensing my confusion.

"Follow me and keep up this time." He was all business. Dressed in slim-cut blue slacks and a tan sweater, he held the door open long enough for me to walk through before he took off.

I kept up the best I could, but it was almost like he was trying to lose me. Every hallway had the same white brick walls, and it seemed as if we were the only two in the building until he pushed open a metal door that read "Talent Only Beyond This Point." We made a right and ran into a crowd of fifty people standing in the narrow hallway. Music was coming from everywhere. Bug stopped at the room with a sign that said "Staff" and opened it.

"Put your bag in here." He said.

"Will it be safe?" I questioned.

"Did you bring sneakers?" He asked, ignoring my question with an eye roll.

"Ugh, yeah, I think."

I'd worn black jeans, a black sweater, and black wedges. All designer shit I couldn't afford because Windell said I needed to "look the part."

"You gotta change into sneakers. You won't make it a day back here with those on."

I picked through the duffle until I found a pair of black Adidas. Bug stood by the door and watched me as I put them on. He didn't give me a chance to tie them before heading back out. He was right. In these, I was able to keep up. Our next stop was Eko's room. Before he opened the door, he turned and looked at me.

"You remember your rules, right?"

"Yes, I said. Don't look Eko in the eye. Don't speak unless spoken to."

"Good. Eko gave you a pass at the club. That don't happen often.

I darted my eyes to the floor and followed behind.

Eko's dressing room had an inch of smoke to pass through before you could see anything. It was surprisingly modest. Two white leather couches sat side by side with a small rectangular glass table in the middle. To the right was a long wooden table flipped over on its side, and food was scattered over the floor.

"I asked for one mother-fucking thing, and y'all couldn't get that right!" Eko screamed.

"I didn't know where to get them..." Addison was pleading with him while trying to clean up the mess I assumed he made

"Hot. Mother-Fucking. Cheetos. Y'all got all this fancy shit, and I asked for Hot. Mother-Fucking. Cheetos." He made sure we felt every word before tossing his Beats by Dre headphones at my feet.

"You have a meet and greet in thirty minutes, bro." Bug intervened

"Fuck that meet and greet!" Eko shot back.

I noticed his tone changed with Bug. Speaking in an even voice, he made sure to not raise it like when he talked to Addison. He spoke to him and not at him.

Bug clenched and unclenched his fists before turning and facing me.

"You need to fix this." He spat at me before leaving the room.

Google is a friend in times of trouble. It took me less than five minutes to find a Chevron near the stadium. I opted to walk rather than wait for the car service. I was back within 15 minutes, holding three bags of hot motherfucking Cheetos.

Addison met me at the door of Eko's room and grabbed the bags without a thank you.

"The dancer's costumes need steaming, and you'll need to help them change in between songs." Addison ordered.

She turned and headed back into the room. Before she could close the door, I heard her high-pitched voice.

"I found the Cheetos Eko!"

Knock. Knock. The dancer's dressing room had a sign that read, "Knock first or regret it later." I opted to knock. After my second tap, the door burst open.

"Hi! I'm Coco!"

Coco was short with curly brown hair that stopped right at her ears. She wore glasses, and based on how she greeted me, I figured she was the outgoing one of the crew.

"Ada." I stuck my right hand out.

"Girl! I hug. Come here!" She said as she grabbed me in a hug and rocked side-to-side.

When she finally released me, I stepped inside. The dancer's dressing room was the complete opposite of Eko's. Though it was small, they made it cozy. It was dimly lit with candles burning in each corner. The only thing that could be heard was the sounds of rain in the background.

A grey sectional surrounded a 50-inch flat-screen perched on the wall. Behind the couch, there were three mirrors set up that I assumed were for practice. Unlike Eko's room, all their food was neatly plated on a round table in the corner.

"This is Andie, Lashae, and Lynne."

The other three girls didn't speak. They kept their seated position on the floor and gave short waves as I walked to the back of the dressing room.

The costumes are over there." Coco pointed.

"They all need to be steamed." Andie interjected.

Andie was what they called a veteran dancer. She'd been on tour with every celebrity worth naming. Andie's hair was long and blonde like Addison's, except her ends were purple. She had bronzed skin that you can tell spent a lot of time in the sun.

"The steamer is on the shelf over there," Lashae added.

I took my cue and grabbed the steamer. The costumes were sleeveless satin leotards with crystals covering the breasts. I can tell everything was hand-stitched.

"Make sure you steam from a distance. The heat can't directly touch the fabric. I would hate for you to have to replace one thousand-dollar costumes."

It was now Lynne's turn to add direction. I could tell I was only going to get along with Coco, and that was fine. At least their dressing room was quiet and drama free. Before I'd left home, Windell told me to focus on making money and not friends. I planned to do just that.

"Showtime ladies." Addison appeared just as I was finishing the last leotard.

"Ada. Bring this rack to the side of the stage and wait. When it's time for them to change, you'll help them out of these shorts and crops."

I was learning not to speak but to only nod my understanding. The dancers left first, and I followed close behind. Standing behind the rack, I pushed it out the dressing room door, only to be pushed backward.

"Ow! Watch where you're going!"

I peeked my head around the rack to find a short, bald man holding a red solo cup. Whatever contents that were inside were now all over his white silk shirt.

"I'm sorry."

"Bitch don't be sorry. Be careful." He barked.

"Bitch?!?" I had been called bitch more times this week than in my whole life. It was time for me to start setting a standard. I stepped around the rack, and before I could tell him where he could put his bitch, the dressing room door across the hall opened.

"Roy! Apologize!"

A shirtless fair-skinned man stood in the doorway. Orange curly hair was wrapped in a man bun on top of his head. Every inch of his skin I could see was tatted. His piercing grey eyes stared at Roy. Roy stood looking conflicted before speaking.

"Sorry." he said before stomping down the hall.

The fair-skinned man winked at me and closed the door.

I made it to the side of the stage just in time to watch the dancers march single file into the dark background. I made sure to push the rack off to the side and watched in awe as they moved in sync. The piercing sound of the crowd could be felt from wherever you stood.

"Y'all ready for Eight?" The DJ yelled.

"Eight.! Eight.! Eight.!" The crowd chanted in unison.

The lights went up, and strobes in different colors danced on the stage floor. The crowd's chants turned into screams as the fair-skinned man who'd I'd just met came out from the other side of the stage. The lights highlighted the ink on his skin in a way I hadn't seen earlier. My eyes followed the snake that started on his wrist and wrapped up his forearm, ending at the base of his neck

"Y'all ready to party?!" He screamed into the mic

The crowd's screams were so loud I could barely hear the words as he began to flow to the beat. Without even realizing it, I'd left the rack behind and started walking closer to the stage. Had I stayed where I was, I probably would have noticed when someone stepped behind me.

"You can't stand here." The voice breathed into my ear.

Chapter 5

"FRANKLY MY DEAR, I DON'T GIVE A FUCK."
- Lucky, Poetic Justice

Startled, I turned to find Bug standing behind me.

"You can either stand behind me or next to me." He said.

He and I were standing toe-toe. I crossed my arms over my chest and turned my head to one side.

"I stand behind no one. Feel free to stand next to me if you'd like."

I made sure to raise my voice so he could hear me over the performance that was still going on behind us. He opened his mouth to say something, but I cut him off by turning my back to him. My focus returnsed to Eight's performance.

"You always this difficult?" He said, moving to stand shoulder to shoulder with me.

"You always bug the shit out of people?" I shot back.

"That's funny," He chuckled.

"Why is that?" I rolled my eyes and unfolded my arms, prepared to give him a piece of my mind if needed.

In a split second, the day's events had turned my inner voice from "remember twenty-five hundred" to "Fuck this job." This was only the first city! My attention never left the stage. Eight had just returned after diving into the crowd. He gave them a farewell wave before heading towards us.

Out the corner of my eye, I could see that Bug was still smirking. He rubbed his hand over his chin and gazed off in the distance as if he remembered something pleasant.

"It's funny because that's how I got my nickname. My mama gave me that name because she said I was always bugging her about something," He said matter-of-factly before walking away.

Eight followed behind him, winking at me and allowing his shoulder to slightly graze mine. Even in the dimly lit place, standing on the side of the stage, his grey eyes still shined bright. I was standing on the side of the stage, his grey eyes still shined bright. Without realizing it, my eyes followed him until he disappeared into his dressing room.

"Water." Andie requested. She took me out of the brief trance Eight had put me in.

She was already dressed in her costume, and the other girls were quickly getting into theirs. I hadn't brought water, and the only place I knew to get it was the dressing room we had just left. Knowing that Eight would be across the hall gave me an unexpected sense of excitement.

"I'll go get it." I said eagerly.

I turned to head back, and the place went completely dark. So dark that I couldn't' see my hand in front of my face. The crowd had begun to chant Eko's name, and the DJ was now silent. Walking wasn't an option, so I opted to stand still. Each side of the stage lit up with fireworks, and Eko appeared in the middle of the stage, sitting at a piano.

He was dressed in a white silk shirt that was being held together with one gold button. His curly hair was braided in two cornrows, and dark shades covered his eyes. He almost looked... normal. Adjusting the mic stand, so it sat just in front of his mouth, he stared at the crowd without saying a word.

The dancers had forgotten their demands and looked on—each adjusting their costumes, preparing for their next moment. Playing soft melodic sounds with his left hand, he used his right to place one finger over his lips. The crowd silenced immediately.

Welcome to my show

This is a private one for you and me

Welcome to my place

Tonight, no matter where you are, you're mine

He softly sang each line, and the crowd went crazy for the simple lyrics. I was amazed at how good he could really sing. Every YouTube video of his was dripping with autotune, but tonight it was just him and the music.

"Wow." I said in awe.

"He's great, isn't he?" Addison said, appearing behind me.

I nodded. The music from the piano had suddenly stopped, and the stage went dark again. The dancers ran to Eko's side. When the lights came up, the piano was gone, and so was Eko's shirt. I was now in my second trance for the night.

"You can't stand here." Addison said, staring at me.

I stared back in confusion.

"Eko's bags will need to be packed and ready to go to the bus. His set is ninety minutes, and you'll need to be done by then. He doesn't like his clothes to touch. So, all shirts in one bag, all pants in another, etc. Everything is labeled. You're smart, so I'm sure you won't have an issue." She explained.

Disappointed that I would be missing the rest of the show, I turned and headed back to Eko's dressing room. When I got to the door, it was locked. Annoyed, I started to head back to Addison when grey eyes opened his dressing room.

"What's your name? He spoke with a southern twang that I couldn't hear when he was rapping.

"Ada." I said.

"I wanted to say sorry about what happened earlier. Let me offer you a drink as a peace offering." Eight said, handing me an opened bottle of Ace of Spades.

"No, thank you." I declined just as Bug was walking up the hallway.

"You need something, Ada?" He asked.

"I need to get into Eko's dressing room, but it's locked."

"I have a key." Bug said, looking at Eight suspiciously.

"After you." I said, gesturing towards the door.

Bug opened the door, and I immediately realized I would need a dream, hope, and prayer to have everything packed in ninety minutes.

"I'll help you." Bug said, reading my mind.

He started at one end of the dressing room, and I jumped at the other. We separated everything into piles and then placed them in the Louis Vuitton luggage Addison had labeled. We worked in silence until I looked up and saw Bug staring at me from across the room.

"What now?" I said.

"Can I give you a piece of advice?" He said, sounding concerned.

I wondered briefly why people always gave you a choice in something they were going to do regardless of what you said. I could tell whatever advice he was going to give was happening whether I said yes or no. I shrugged my shoulders anyway.

"This tour isn't the place to make friends. Especially with any artists, and that includes Eko. Be careful."

We managed to finish packing up for Eko just in time for him to finish his set. Addison walked into the dressing room and looked pleased. We had a total of seven bags.

"Good job, Ada." She squeaked.

Bug smirked from the corner but didn't give away the fact that he'd split the work with me. Satisfied with what I had done, I headed to find my bag and get some much-needed sleep on our ride to the next city.

"Where are you going?" Addison asked.

"I'm going to grab my bag and get on the bus." I said, stopping at the doorway.

"Oh, no." She protested.

"These bags will need to be carried to Eko's bus personally."

"We don't have help with that?" I questioned.

Addison and Bug stared at each other as if I had asked my question in French. Their eyes shared an understanding that I wasn't privy to. I wanted to repeat myself, but before I could, they both let out the loudest laughs.

"Do we have help for that?" Addison said, mocking me.

"YOU are the help!" Bug said, leaning over the couch in hysterics.

Being called the help didn't sit right with me. I was glad Bug had said it and not Addison. Had a white girl called me the help, this would have been an entirely different scene. They were both still laughing when I walked over and picked up two of the duffle bags. They each felt like they weighed twenty pounds, but I made sure not to react to the extra weight in any way.

I couldn't give them the satisfaction of knowing carrying seven of these was going to kill me. I didn't make eye contact with either of them as I left the room to find the tour bus.

"The tour bus is straight out the back door." Addison called behind me.

Her laughs floated through the halls as I walked out the back door. Once it closed, I dropped both bags and let my favorite fingers fly. Even if they couldn't see, it made me feel better. Finding which bus was Eko's didn't cause me much trouble. There were only two parked behind the building.

One was all black with blue lights shining underneath. It was forty feet long, and Eko's face was plastered on one side. In the picture, he was holding a blunt, and the smoke he blew cascaded up the side of the bus. If I didn't know any better, I would have thought it was a hologram. The bus directly behind it was half the size of Eko's.

It was an awful yellow color and had the words "The Help" scribbled across one side. I rolled my eyes to the sky, realizing that this would be my home for the remainder of the tour. The luggage compartment under Eko's bus was open, so I threw both bags in and started back for the rest. I opened the back door and saw Bug walking towards me with two more of the bags we packed.

"Looks like you're the help, too." I said with a smirk.

"I'm whatever I need to be when I need to be it. Right now, I'm helping you." Bug made sure to stretch out the helping part as he walked past me to the bus.

"I got it. You don't have to help."

"Oh. Yes, I do. I saw you struggling with the two you picked up, and I can see from here you put both bags in the wrong place."

"Wrong place?"

"The bags go on the bus and not beneath it."

Like a toddler having a fit, I stomped back to the bus and picked up the two bags I'd just left. Bug had already started up the stairs, and I followed behind.

"You should always put all of his luggage in his bedroom. Pile it neatly to the right so Addison can put out whatever he needs."

The inside of Eko's bus spared no expense. The floors were marble, and all the furniture was cream to match the stone countertops. There was a full kitchen, living room area, and six bunk beds before you made it to the master suite in the back. The master is where Bug dropped his two bags and then reached back for mine. I handed them over while examining the inside of the bedroom. The master's inside had a king-size bed, full bathroom, and two 65in tv's to match the two we'd already passed.

"You ready to get the rest of the bags?" Bug said, stopping my inspection.

"So, can I ask you a question?" I said as we stepped off the bus.

From behind, I could see his head shake in agreeance.

"What do you do here?"

"What needs to be done." He said, chuckling.

"So, you're the third assistant." I said with a chuckle of my own.

"Eko and I have been best friends since grade school - so like any friend, I'm whatever he needs when he needs it. Assistant, security, enforcer, you name it."

We'd made it back to Eko's dressing room as he was leaving the stage. He was walking in our direction, drenched in sweat. He gave Bug a head nod before disappearing inside. Addison was trailing behind, clicking on her phone. She looked up to see me and motioned for me to come over.

"Are the bags on the bus?"

"We - I mean I, have three more bags," I said, cutting my eye at Bug before he retreated into the dressing room.

It was just now that Addison decided to look up from her phone at me. She looked aggravated, and I could tell the next words out of her mouth weren't going to be excellent. I braced myself for an exchange, but to my surprise, she glanced over my shoulder then back at me. I turned around to see Bug holding all three bags. He tipped his head at us and walked down the hall without another word.

"Grab your bags and head to your bus. It's the yellow one behind ours. I will brief you in the next city." She said, confirming my earlier suspicion about my living quarters. Her direction didn't require a response, so I moved past her, searching for the room I'd left my belongings.

I wanted to ask Addison where she'd be staying, but the "ours" in her sentence told me all I needed to know. After a few wrong turns, I found the room. When I picked up my duffle and slung it over my shoulder, a small note dropped by my foot. I picked it up and admired the neat handwriting.

You owe me one. – Bug

Chapter 6

"I'M SURPRISED YOU'RE NOT BRUISED FROM ALL THE WOMEN THROWING THEMSELVES AT YOU."

– Kyle Barker, Living Single

That night on "The Help," I slept horribly. It wasn't unusual. Since Amare died, sleep never came easy. My dreams were either of us in happier times or a replay of me laying with him as he took his last breath. Tonight, we were on our first date. The restaurant was always full of people, but in the dream, I could only hear us. We were laughing non-stop until suddenly, I knocked over a glass of red wine.

I left to clean myself up, but when I returned, the restaurant was empty. In Amare's place, there was only a note. I could never read the words. Sweat had the fabric from my t-shirt, sticking to my body when I awoke. Alarmed, I breathed deep to settle my nerves. After some time, my eyes adjusted to the darkness, and I remembered where I was. Though the bus was half the size of Eko's, it was clean and warm.

The girls weren't very talkative, and I was grateful. We each had our own bunk, and we shared one bathroom. Our living room area had two couches and our kitchen just a sink and microwave. I rolled over to check my phone. 3:30am. This meant we were only an hour away from our next city. We would be in Charlotte, NC, for one night only.

I learned from the girls that we'd travel non-stop to each city, only stopping for gas. Addison had made sure to text around midnight with instructions for when we arrived. In search of peace, I grabbed the latest book by Eric Jerome Dickey and hoped being lost in his world would give me a break from mine. As I flipped the pages, the note from Bug fell to my lap.

I re-read the words twice.

"You owe me one." I whispered.

I pondered its meaning. I was hoping Bug didn't think that carrying bags to the bus entitled him to anything. Admiring his neat handwriting, I decided to not throw it away. Instead, I tucked it neatly in the front pane of the book. I only got two sentences in before I dozed off. When I finally got into a dreamless sleep, the bus came to an abrupt stop.

Opening the blinds, the lights in front of The Ritz Carlton shined bright inside the bus. The hotel was lit in blue and made of all glass. It stood six stories high, overlooking the whole city. Climbing down from my bunk, I snuggled into the living room couch to get a better look. Eko had just made it to the front entrance, where a concierge was eagerly waiting. Taking the glass of champagne waiting for him, Eko disappeared inside.

"Ada."

I heard my name through the front doors of the bus. Her high-pitched voice startled the driver, and he quickly pressed the button to open the doors.

Addison stood on the other side. Closing my eyes, I mentally prepared before stepping down to meet her.

"Eko's bags need to be brought up to the room." Addison said with no greeting at all.

I didn't dare ask why the hotel staff wouldn't be bringing his bags up. It hadn't even struck five am, but Addison was fully dressed. Her makeup was subtle, and she was dressed in casual wear. It was the first time I had seen her wear sneakers. I looked down at my terry cloth pajamas and plain white crop top. I hadn't even showered.

"Let me just grab a pair of sweats." I said.

"No time. Grab the bags. You can change later."

She gave me no time, so I grabbed my sneakers and walked over to the bus. Bug was sleeping peacefully on one of the couches when I walked up. I made sure to tip-toe to the room and grab the first two bags.

The concierge had pulled a luggage cart up, and I loaded every bag without waking Bug. Eko's presidential suite sat on the twenty-first floor. I had been given a unique code to enter the elevator and a keycard for the room. I stepped off the elevator to find Eight waiting.

"You need help?" He said, eyeing the luggage cart.

"No. Thank you." I smirked.

His grey eyes had now turned blue in this light. With one hand, he held the elevator door open as I pushed the bags through. Out the corner of my eye, I could see his eyes linger as I continued down the hall. Directing my focus to the end of the hall, I could hear music coming from the presidential suite. Instead of the loud trap music I had been used to hearing, there was soft R&B music floating from the door.

I used my key to let myself in and immediately regretted it.

"Ada!"

If it hadn't been for the squeak of her high-pitched voice, I wouldn't have known it was her. I was frozen with my right foot propping the door and my left hand on the luggage cart. Addison was naked on all fours. Her blonde hair was nearly covering her face, and behind her, Eko was standing at full attention. We all paused in awkward silence.

"You can join us if you want?" Eko laughed.

The laugh reminded me that this was not a movie or a dream. I stumbled my way backward, slamming the door behind. Just before it closed, I could hear Eko shout.

"Come back in 15 minutes."

I pushed the luggage to the right side of the door. Standing against the wall on the other side, I slid my body to the floor. What else could I do but wait? I hadn't been given a room assignment, and I damn sure wasn't towing these bags back down the elevator. Dropping my hands in my head, I hoped I could at least nap. The ding from the elevator ended that plan.

Bug stepped off the elevator with a bag in each hand. As he got closer, I could see that one of them was mine. He handed me the bag without a word. I took it and expressed my thanks with a smile. Before walking off, he looked from the door to the luggage and then back at me. The song behind the doors had just changed to Focus by HER.

"That's song number five. You only got about five more minutes to wait." Bug said with a chuckle.

I dropped my head in my hands for a second time as he walked away.

That night backstage went a lot smoother than the night before. Every seat in Bank of America Stadium was filled, and the entire stadium flashed in lights of blue. I stood next to Bug for the whole performance, and to my surprise, he didn't speak much. The show ended an hour ahead of schedule, and Eko stepped off stage, drenched in sweat.

"Aye. Yo. Brenden. I saw something." He panted.

"Where?" Bug said, stepping closer to the stage and moving the curtain to the side.

"Black Bodysuit. Long black hair. Front row." He said with a smile from ear-to-ear.

Bug seemed to make out who he was looking for and nodded his approval.

"Take her with you." Eko said, pointing at me.

I had been purposely ignoring their conversation until I heard my name.

"Take me where?" I said.

"Follow me. I'll explain on the way." Bug said.

Not waiting for me to inquire further, he practically ran from behind the stage. Starting a light jog was the only way I could keep up with his pace. We bypassed the dressing rooms and headed towards the front of the venue. Bug slowed his pace a little as we got closer to the stadium seats, and I finally got a chance to speak.

"Brenden?" I asked.

"My real name. You call me Bug." He said, cutting his eye at me.

"What did he see?" I said, wanting to change the subject.

"Something for the night."

I had no idea what that meant, but we were now standing in the middle of a large number of people trying to exit. We pushed through them until we reached the first two rows. Bug's eyes darted the rows, looking for the needle in the haystack.

"There she is." He pointed. "I need you to go over there and tell her Eko has requested her for the night."

"What?!?!" I said.

"They feel more comfortable when a girl asks." He explained with a shrug.

I figured this must be a hazing moment. This was a test on how much the new girl was willing to do. Bug's face said that this was an earnest request. He even looked at his watch to let me know we didn't have much time. I was sure that no woman would go anywhere with a stranger "for the night."

Especially when he's sending some random girl to ask for him. I marched over to Black Bodysuit with that confidence. Fully prepared to turn around and prove to Bug how ridiculous he was being. She'd just exited her row and stood in the aisle by the time I made it to her.

"Hi. I like your bodysuit." I said, trying to break the ice.

"Thanks." She said in a dry tone while looking me up and down.

She wasn't interested in having any further conversation with me. There was no smooth way to pick up a girl for someone else, so I laid it all on the line.

"I work with Eko, and he has requested you."

Nervousness dripped from my voice. Black bodysuit was only silent for a moment before a piercing scream escaped her lips.

"He picked me! He picked me!" She said over and over. The anti-social vixen was now full of life.

Once she was done leaping for joy, I motioned for her to follow me back to where Bug was waiting.

"What do we do with her now?" I said, rolling my eyes.

"We vet her." He said with a smirk.

Black Bodysuit blindly followed us backstage, leaving all three of her friends behind. I asked her twice if she was sure. The second time Bug pinched my arm lightly to request my silence. Backstage was vacant except for the few members of the cleaning crew when we returned.

"We need to make this quick." Bug said, taking the lead.

"I need to see your ID before we go anywhere." He held out his hand.

Black Bodysuit dug in the back pocket of her jeans and handed him her driver's license. How Eko had laid eyes on her in a crowd of thousands left me perplexed. She barely stood over five feet tall. Once her heels were off, I'm sure she was even closer to the ground. Looking at her now, I could tell she was barely over 21. Hair flowing down her back and cocoa-colored skin, she could be my sister if I had one.

Handing her back the license, Bug didn't seem to care. Satisfied with what he read, he pulled out a small piece of paper from his suit jacket and gave it to her.

"Sign this. It's a consent form." He said, handing her a pen.

She didn't read a line of it before scribbling her name on the bottom.

"So, where is he?" She said, eagerly handing the paper back to him.

Bug didn't answer her question. He just turned to walk towards the exit. A sprinter van was waiting for us behind the building, and we both hopped in after him. Black bodysuit sat in the front and immediately started touching up her makeup. In the back, Bug sat next to me.

"When we get to the hotel, take her to room 1227 and leave her." He instructed.

"And leave her?" I repeated.

Sensing the panic in my eyes. Bug placed one hand on my shoulder.

"Relax. We aren't sex trafficking this girl. She's an adult and choosing to have a one-night stand with a celebrity. Loosen up. You'll get used to this."

Get used to this. I never think I could. However, Bug had a point. She was making a choice, and we were doing a job. At the hotel, we traveled up to the top floor. The only person uneasy was me. Bug pulled me to the side as soon as we stepped off. He stepped in close to me and spoke in a whisper.

"My room is across the hall. Next door to the presidential suite. We've rented this whole floor. If she decides to leave, she won't get back in. You got this?"

Finishing his instruction, he handed me a room key. Agitated, I moved my head up and down to signal my understanding. Returning to Black Bodysuit's side, I opened the room door and escorted her in. Placing the room key on the side of the bed, I asked again if she would like anything.

"Can I order room service?" She asked wide-eyed.

I gave her a thumbs up. Lingering in the corner, I hoped she might change her mind before I left. Instead, she looked annoyed at my presence. Not one to stay where I'm not wanted, I wished her a good night. Giving a reminder that my room was just next door.

The room I had been assigned was nothing compared to the two-bedroom suite I had dropped Eko's luggage off to earlier. It would still do the job for tonight. I stripped my clothes and started the shower. Setting it to the hottest temperature, I allowed the steam to create my own personal sauna. I sent Windell a quick text to let him know everything was going well before getting up to step under the hot water.

I hadn't stepped ona foot onto the tile floor before I heard loud screams. My first instinct was to mind my business until the shrieks were followed by a loud crash. Turning off the shower, I could tell the sounds were coming from next door. My thoughts immediately went to Black Bodysuit.

Thinking the worst, I grabbed my robe to investigate.

Chapter 7

"HE'S A DOG. TAIL-HAVING, ANYTHING-THAT-MOVES-HUMPING-ASS-DOG!"

– Shante, Two Can Play That Game

As I got closer to room 1227, the screams got louder. The door was slightly open, so I pushed my way in. Eko was standing in between Black Bodysuit and Addison. The room had been trashed. Stepping over two lamps and piles of glass, I looked on in awe.

Black Bodysuit was naked except for the sheet she was holding to cover the front of her body. The makeup she'd worked so hard on was now smeared, and her skin was painted with scratches. Addison was holding a vase over her head, preparing to throw it in their direction. I stayed at the door.

"You're fucking another bitch right down the hall from me!" She screamed at the top of her lungs. The vase still hadn't left her hand. Eko and his guest cringed every time she moved.

"Addison, please put down the vase." I tried to reason with her from my spot at the door.

The look she shot back at me said the time for reasoning had long passed.

"It's not what it looks like." Eko tried to explain.

That age-old lie was enough to send her over the edge. The vase went flying. Both Eko and the young girl dived to opposite sides before it shattered into pieces between them. Leaving them distracted, Addison found her opening to lunge at Black Bodysuit. Her fist landed right in Black Bodysuit's right eye.

Landing on top of her, Addison went for another punch before Bug barged in. Grabbing Addison and hoisting her over his shoulder, he eyed us all.

"What the fuck is going on in here?!" He screamed.

Bug's eyes dashed from me to the door. I realized then that it had been open this whole time. Closing it, I signaled for Black Bodysuit to come to me. When she was close enough, I examined her right eye. Bug looked to Eko for an explanation. He offered a shrug in return. Addison's sobs were all we heard next.

"I can't believe this!" She screamed from over Bug's bare shoulder.

I started to analyze his body instead of tending to the bruising, starting to form around Black Bodysuit's eye. From the clothing he wore, I could tell he was in good shape. Seeing him, shirtless confirmed it. I instinctively licked my lips.

"Put me down!" Addison demanded.

Her sobs had slowed, and it seemed she had calmed down. Even so, Bug waited a few seconds before slowly lowering her. Once her feet touched the ground, she marched out of the room.

Realizing there was nothing more I could do for the girl inside the room, I chose to follow Addison. Leaving Bug to clean up whatever mess was left.

"You okay?" I asked as we stepped inside the suite.

Looking at her red face, a wave of guilt fell over me. Though I had only done what I was asked, I still played a part in her heartbreak. The way she inspected my face as she threw her luggage on the bed made me feel like she knew.

"You should make arrangements to get home tomorrow." She said in a low voice.

Was she firing me? Standing in disbelief, I wanted to protest. There had only been two cities, and I hadn't even gotten paid yet. Addison looked up, and her face showed surprise that I was still standing there.

"You can go." She said with the wave of her arm.

I didn't feel it was worth debating. Heading back towards my room, I saw Bug escorting Eko's failed one night stand to the elevators. She'd gotten dressed and pulled her long hair in a bun. Before leaving, Bug handed her a wad of money. Snatching it from his hands, she was gone. Back in my room, I tossed the small numbers of clothes I'd unpacked back into my bag. Taking a deep breath, I started another text to Windell.

> I need help getting home. Sorry.

I woke up the next morning, fully clothed. I wanted to be sure all I would need to do is get up and go. The clock next to the bed read 6:30 am. Checking my phone, I saw that I had received a response from Windell just an hour before.

> Check your bag. You can tell me the rest later.

His message confused me, but I headed over to my duffle bag anyway. Taking every bit of clothing out. I started to feel around. To my surprise, there was a small compartment sewn in the side of my luggage. I unzipped it and found an envelope with the words "If the shit hits the fan" written on it. Inside were ten one-hundred-dollar bills. Letting out a low squeal, I repacked my bag.

Wanting to leave with an ounce of dignity, I eased out of my hotel room and closed the door lightly. I had never experienced being fired, and I didn't plan on the first time being by a high maintenance celebrity.

"Ada."

I heard my name being called as I headed toward the elevator. It was a voice I didn't recognize. Deep and raspy.

"Ada." it called again.

Turning around, Eko was standing outside of his presidential suite in a long white robe. His head motioned for me to follow him inside. If it hadn't been for the desperation in his eyes, I would have ignored him completely. He looked like he hadn't slept. His red eyes and the knotted hair on top of his head told me there had to be something more.

Walking in the room, my suspicion was proved right. The inside of the suite was destroyed. Furniture had been turned over, and every drink in the minibar had been opened and poured on the bed. Anything that wasn't nailed down had been broken.

"She took everything." Eko said softly.

The confident public figure was now a shell of a man. Surveying the room, two watches, two Cuban link chains, and two bracelets remained on the dresser. Addison had written LIAR. CHEATER. ASSHOLE. in big letters on the floor-length mirror with lipstick.

"Where were you?" I asked in disbelief.

"I stayed in Bug's room. I thought she just needed time to cool off."

He was now sitting on the edge of the California king-sized bed, resting his chin in his hands. The end of his sentence trailed off, and he began staring at the empty closet across from him. The place I had hung all his clothes yesterday was now bare.

"Did she take your clothes?" I said, asking the obvious.

"I need you to go get me something to wear to the next city. We can figure the rest out when we get to DC." He ordered in return.

In an instant, his big shot personality had returned.

"We? I thought I was fired?"

"Fired? You just got promoted. Now go."

He shoved an American Express Black card into my hand and reminded me I only had an hour. I didn't have time to wrap my mind around what promotion meant before heading out the door.

"Bug is going with you." He called after me.

Bug was already waiting by the elevator when I got there.

"I have a car that can take us to Concord Mills Mall." He said, gesturing for me to enter the elevator ahead of him.

"Do you know what I'm supposed to get? I asked once we'd gotten inside the privacy of the elevator.

It had just dawned on me that I didn't know the first thing about shopping for a man–especially one that was as flashy as Eko. I wore designer clothing only when Windell bought it for me, and Amare preferred to buy his own clothes. As for me, I spent most of my adult life in scrubs. When I wasn't in scrubs, I was in what my brother would call 'Plain Jane' wear.

"We will just have to figure it out together."

Bug gave me a reassuring smile just as the elevator opened to the lobby. Outside, an all-black SUV was waiting for us.

"Concord Mills Mall." Bug instructed the driver once we were inside.

The ride to Concord Mills Mall was silent. There were a few times I caught Bug looking at me, but he never said a word. After his third glance, I broke the silence.

"What? You have more advice for me?"

"Nah. Just thinking that you handled yourself well last night. Most people would have freaked out."

"I've seen far worse in the ER."

"ER?"

"Yeah. I was an ER nurse in a previous life."

His face was stunned. I could see the wheels turning. He was probably asking himself, why would someone from my background be babysitting a demanding celebrity. I'm sure he had many questions, but as we pulled up to the mall, I needed to make it clear that they wouldn't be answered.

"No, I don't want to talk about it." I said flatly.

The driver opened the door, and we stepped out. I was grateful that Bug didn't push the issue. Concord Mills Mall was a tourist attraction disguised as a shopping center. There were over two hundred stores, and we were no closer to figuring out where to go while standing in front of the digital directory.

"There are no designer stores here." I pointed.

Bug scrolled the directory for a third time, hoping that Versace, Gucci, or Louis Vuitton would pop up out of nowhere. I nervously checked my watch. We now had less than 45 minutes to get back to the hotel. I scanned the floor we were on and saw H&M.

"Let's go." I called after Bug.

"He isn't going to wear this." Bug said as we entered the store.

"He really just needs something to wear to the new city. We are going to buy from this store, take the tags off and tell him it's a new up and coming designer."

I was trying to think quickly on my feet. Eko didn't really know the difference between a high-end designer and regular everyday clothing. Most celebrities just buy it because it's expensive. Bug and I chose to divide and conquer inside the store. I sent him to the side with loungewear bottoms, and I found the area with basic tee-shirts.

We met back at the register in under 10 minutes. Our total came to $50, and Bug joked that Eko's socks usually cost more than this. Our next stop was Footaction. We picked up two pairs of Nikes and made it back to the car with only 20 minutes to get back to the hotel. While we rode, I pulled the tags off each piece of clothing. Bug watched while shaking his head.

"I hope for your sake this works." He laughed.

I rolled my eyes and stuffed the clothes in a plain bag I managed to find on our way out the door. Having the emergency money, eased my worry of if this would work or not. I made a mental note to send Windell half of my first paycheck should I make it through the next few cities.

"You miss it?" Bug was staring at me again.

"Miss what?" I said as we pulled up to the front of the hotel.

"Being a nurse. You miss it?"

"Not at all." I said before rushing to get out of the car.

Eko seemed none the wiser when I handed him the bag of clothes. He inspected the basic clothes we'd purchased and then slipped into the bathroom. I gave Bug a quick grin. When Eko came out, he looked at me.

"What brand is this?"

"Ummm... It's a new designer, but we didn't catch the name" I stumbled over my lie.

Bug covered his mouth to conceal his laughter. Eko touched the t-shirt, then the pants. He did that three times in the mirror then looked back at us suspiciously.

"It feels real H&M-ish, but it will do for the ride," He said, sliding on a pair of black shades and heading out the room.

Bug could no longer cover his laugh, and I couldn't help but join in.

All four dancers were waiting as I got to the bus. They wasted no time grilling me about Addison. Needing to vent, I shared all I knew. At the end of my story, the bus fell quiet.

"DAMN!" They said in unison.

"Well, at least you still got a job." Coco chimed in.

"Addison fired the last three, so I'm surprised you even made it this long." Lynne followed.

Andie had grown unimpressed with our gossip session and retreated to her bunk. We still hadn't pulled out of the Ritz's parking lot. I briefly wondered what the hold up was but soon climbed into my bunk. Though it was only the middle of the day, sleep found me. I was dreaming of being wrapped in Amare's arms before my body started to shake.

My eyes popped open to find Bug leaning over my bunk.

"Get up. You're on the wrong bus." He said before disappearing.

Startled, I climbed down from my bunk and followed Bug. We walked to Eko's bus, and Bug tapped twice on the doors before they opened.

"Where have you been?" Eko asked.

"I went to my bus. Did you need anything else from me?" I questioned.

"This is your bus now. Make yourself at home."

With that, Eko went back to his room in the back of the bus.

"I'll grab your bag." Bug offered.

I looked around the bus and remembered that I needed to respond to Windell.

> False alarm. Looks like I live to fight another day.

Chapter 8

"WELL, WE'RE MOVIN' ON UP. TO THE EASTSIDE. TO A DELUXE APARTMENT IN THE SKY."
– *The Jeffersons*

Eko's bus was far less peaceful than 'The Help'. Even though it was bigger and much more superior. A little after the first hour, it was filled with weed smoke. Music played at constant loud levels, and every light remained on through the night. It was a good thing that I usually didn't sleep well because there was none to be had here.

Bug opted to sleep on the couch, and I had my pick of bunks. My eyes were wide open for most of the six-and-a-half-hour drive to Washington, D.C. A surge of relief washed over me when I felt the bus come to a stop. Lifting the blinds, I had a view of The Four Seasons. The high building was made completely of brick. You wouldn't be able to tell it housed rooms that started at over $800 a night from the outside.

The bus crept around the building before coming to another stop at the back entrance. I sat up straight in my bunk, waiting for my first direction. Instinctively, I checked my watch–8:30 pm. The show wasn't scheduled until tomorrow night. Now I was hoping that meant I would be able to catch up on the rest I'd lost. Bug peeked his eyes open and glance over at me from the couch.

"What do you think they're waiting on?" I asked.

I could see from the window that two concierges stood out front, patiently waiting for our arrival. One held a tray of champagne glasses, while the other stood between two large empty luggage carts. They were anxiously looking from bus to bus.

"You." Bug answered me.

"Me?" I asked.

Bug rolled his eyes at my uncertainty.

"You're going to need to catch up quick. In every city, you need to be off the bus first. Check Eko in and get a room list from the front desk." He instructed.

Hurrying down from my bunk, I went out to meet the concierge. He handed me a glass of champagne, which I happily accepted. I think I could get used to this treatment.

"Are you Ada?" He asked.

"Yes, I am."

"Someone called ahead and said you'd be taking care of the check-in process. Right, this way." He grabbed the bag I was carrying and led me to the front desk.

The check-in process was easy enough. I got to make up an alias for Eko to stay under. Choosing a female name would be harder to guess. Today he would be Toni Jackson. A mix of my two favorite female entertainers. After giving the dancers their room assignments, I went to collect Eko.

He and Bug were already waiting. Handing Bug his keycard, I rushed to the back to collect Eko's bags. To my surprise, the bags were all gone.

"Where are your bags?" I called.

"The hotel staff grabbed them." Bug answered for Eko.

"I don't know why you were bringing them up to my room. That's why we pay to stay in nice hotels." Eko laughed.

Well, I'll be damned. Cursing Addison in my head, I followed them off the bus, and we entered a private elevator to The Royal Suite. Once inside, Bug wished us a good night and headed off to find his own room.

The Royal Suite was definitely fit for a king. A lounge area with its own marble fireplace welcomed us when we walked in. Blue and white couches circled around a stone coffee table. The room was larger than most homes in the area. Continuing my room survey, I entered the master suite with a full white marble bathroom and its own terrace.

There was a single king-sized bed, a love seat, and two couches. They chose subtle tones for the master, which included grey and white undertones. Just as Eko and Bug had informed me, all his luggage was neatly piled in the right corner. They'd even gone so far as to hang his clothing in the walk-in closet.

My work for the night appeared to be done. I found Eko sitting in the library of the suite. Yes, there was a library. He was using a tray table to sprinkle weed in a light white paper. Soft Jazz was playing overhead.

"Do you need anything else from me this evening?" I asked.

"Nah. You good." He said, using his tongue to seal the blunt.

I nodded and turned to leave before realizing that my name wasn't listed on the check-in list.

"I didn't get a room number." I said.

He took a long pull of the blunt he'd just rolled and blew smoke in the air.

"You got promoted. This is your room number." He said with a smirk.

My face filled with worry and concern. I knew first hand what Eko was used to with Addison. I was staring at him, trying to find the words to tell him I was not her. Picking up on my apprehension. He explained further.

"As my executive assistant, you'll always stay with me. You can leave your bags in here and share the closet if you want. As far as sleeping arrangements – "

He'd risen from his seat and started towards the master suite.

"You can choose the love seat or bed. Your choice." He grinned.

Standing in the middle of his master bedroom, he gestured at the couches and then back at the bed like a game show host. It made sense. Everything was a game to him.

"I'll choose the living room." I spat.

He didn't get a chance to confirm or deny my choice before I rushed off to the living room area. Exploring, I found extra blankets and sheets hidden in a small cabinet inside the library. I was no stranger to a makeshift bed. A couch in a room costing $7,500 a night would feel as good as any bed.

Flopping onto the couch felt like heaven. I wrapped myself in the down comforter and rested my eyes. Forcing myself to sleep became even more difficult with every light in the room being on. Hopping up, I began to flip every switch. My last stop was the bedroom.

Eko was sound asleep when I tiptoed in. I barely rested my hand on the light switch before he popped his eyes open.

"Don't turn it off." He mumbled.

"The light?" I questioned.

"Yeah, the light. I can't sleep in the dark."

I wanted to ask why a grown man couldn't sleep in the dark or alone in a suite for that matter, but I decided against it. Heading back to my area, I heard two faint knocks on the door. Looking through the peephole, I saw no one. As I started to walk away, I noticed a small piece of paper slipped under the door.

Room J112. Midnight.

The "J" stood for Junior suite. I knew that room belonged to Bug. Laying back down on the couch, I wondered what the note was summoning me to. Eko's snores were floating throughout the suite as I contemplated ignoring the message. I tossed and turned for a bit before curiosity got the best of me. There was something mysterious about Bug that I wanted to investigate further.

Hoping that my invitation was a platonic one, I didn't see the need to change my sweats and oversized t-shirt. I checked Eko's room once again before sneaking out. As I tip-toed down the hall, I giggled at how ridiculous I was being.

A grown woman was sneaking down a quiet hallway like a teenager sneaking out past curfew. I could hear laughs and soft music coming from behind Bug's door. I knocked twice and waited awhile before I hit the door again. The door swung open, following my second knock.

"Heyyyyyy!" Coco slurred.

She reached out and pulled me into a big hug. Though she'd always been friendly, I haven't experienced her being this warm. I reluctantly squeezed her back and stepped past her into the suite. Bug's room was filled with people. It had a view of D.C. that we didn't share in the Royal Suite.

His living room, though smaller, had fit ten people comfortably. I recognized the other three dancers huddled to themselves in the corner, but the rest of the faces were unfamiliar.

"Welcome!" Bug called from the corner.

He stepped over a few people to make his way to me.

"Can I get you a drink?" He asked eagerly.

"Yes!" My voice was more ecstatic than I had planned.

He seemed to not notice as we made our way over to the kitchen area. I took a seat at the island while he grabbed a silver shaker and added liquor without asking my preference. I watched him pick through mixers and garnishes. He was in his element.

"Check you out." I faked applause.

"I used to bartend in college." He said.

"You went to college?" I asked surprised.

Stopping mid shake, he rolled his eyes at me. Unknowingly, I had hit a sore spot. He lowered his eyes and leaned towards me over the island.

"You're not the only educated one." He hissed.

Carefree Bug had now disappeared again. I added college to the mental list of things not to bring up around Bug and watched in silence as he continued to put the finishing touches on the drink. Instead of his typical suit and tie look, he was casual. He paired his black jeans with a t-shirt that said, "Black Women Love Me." I laughed out loud at that.

"What's so funny?" Bug said, pouring the drink in a glass.

"Just wondering what permission you got from the black women delegation to wear that shirt."

He chuckled. That seemed to break the ice a little, and he slid the drink over to me. I picked up the cocktail glass and took the cherry garnish in my mouth.

"What's this called?" I asked after my first sip.

"Manhattan. Figured with all your education, you'd know that." He said with a grin.

"Touché"

"Make yourself at home. Everyone here works for or with Eko. We just like to have a little kickback on the off days."

Bug had taken the seat next to me with his own drink in hand.

"I know the dancers. Who are the others? I asked.

"A few stagehands and band members. They normally travel separately from us."

I nodded my head in understanding and continued to sip slowly on my drink. Looking around the room, I noticed Lynne was starting to gather everyone into the living room.

"Story Time!" She yelled.

"Oh! Pick me!" Coco's hand shot straight in the air.

"Let's talk about the time that Eko walked out of a show because his dressing room wasn't set to 78 degrees!" She falls over with laughter at that thought.

"Or – "Lynne started.

"What about the time we couldn't perform because his dressing room was supposed to be all eggshell white. When we walked in, he swore the couch was more of an off-white and refused to perform."

The whole room erupted in laughter for that story. Bug listened as everyone shared their own horrific Eko experience but never shared any of his own. Once my Manhattan was finished, he took my glass without prompt and made me another. He did that three more times before the night ended. I hadn't drunk this much in a long time, but I was grateful for the peace the buzz was giving me.

"You good?" Bug tapped the island to grab my attention.

"Yeah, why?"

"You've had that silly smile plastered on your face for ten minutes." He said with a chuckle.

My whiskey vision didn't realize that the room had cleared out and the only people left were Bug and me. He had started picking up the living room, and I felt obligated to help.

"Why don't you let housekeeping do this?" I said as I picked up empty glasses and plates.

"My mother was a housekeeper, so I don't want them to do any more than they have to. I even make the bed before I leave." He said.

"That's sweet." I said, placing the trash I had collected in the bag he held open for me.

"Can I ask you a question?" He said before I could turn around to finish cleaning.

"Do I have a choice?" I grinned.

"You do."

"Go ahead."

"Did you like being a nurse?"

"I did. It was my greatest gift to be able to help people. Even those who didn't make it, I always did what I could to make them comfortable."

"Being a doctor was my dream. Always wanted to know what it felt like to save a life."

"So why didn't you?" Now it was my turn to ask the questions.

"Right after college, my mother was diagnosed with cancer. I went home to take care of her. Took two years, but she recovered. Eko was right by my side through the whole thing. Around the time we found out she was cancer-free, Eko started to get a little buzz in the streets. When he asked me to be head of security, I couldn't turn him down. I felt like I owed him."

"I hope your loyalty will be rewarded." That was all I could offer in response.

"I hope so too." He said with a sigh.

"Let me load your dishwasher, and I'll be on my way." I proposed.

"Nah. I will take care of this tomorrow. I am going to bed."

"At least you have a bed." I said back.

Even I could hear the jealousy in my voice.

"Tell Eko he owes me $100." He laughed, holding the door open for me.

"Why?" I asked, confused.

"Told him you'd choose the couch."

His comment brought my favorite finger out of retirement. I shot one at him and left the room. I could still hear him laughing as I walked down the hall. Though I wanted to be annoyed, once I was nestled in my homemade sleeping bag on the couch, I laughed too.

Chapter 9
"YOU GOTTA COORDINATE!"
– Mr. Jackson, Boomerang

My senses woke me up to the unmistakable smell of something burning. I sat straight up on the couch and I coughed twice. The smoke was already starting to fill up the room. Panic began to set in.

"Eko!" I screamed, hopping up.

I ran to the bedroom, which was empty, and then to the office. Eko was nowhere to be found. The 4,000 square foot room turned into a maze. I zig-zagged through rooms I hadn't managed to see the night before. My fight or flight was telling me every man for himself. The decency in me said I would regret a headline reading "R&B singer dies in hotel room fire. Assistant survives after leaving him for dead". My last turn took me past the terrace. The door was open.

The terrace was damp from morning dew. Though it was summer, I shivered from the cool morning breeze. Just outside, Eko was standing over a small grill with a long white robe on. When he turned to see me, he smiled.

"Ada. I'm making bacon. You want some?"

He held up a piece of black crumbled bacon for my inspection.

"You're burning bacon!" I shouted from the other side of the door.

How hadn't the smoke alarms gone off, I thought.

"Nah. Bacon ain't done till it's burnt. Room service bacon is never crispy enough for me, so I always have them bring me a grill." He scoffed.

"That sounds nice, but you need to turn that off before the smoke alarms go off. Then the whole fire department will be up here."

As the words left my mouth, the loud siren of the smoke alarm filled the room behind us. Loud bangs came from the front door immediately. Fearing that they would kick in the door, I ran to open it. Bug was standing on the other side of the door with three of the hotel's staff.

"Everything okay in here?" he huffed.

"Yes, we are fine. Eko was cooking bacon." I said, lowering my eyes in embarrassment.

The hotel staff showed a look of relief as they went in and reset the smoke detectors. Bug plopped down on the couch opposite mine and watched them work. Silence came within ten minutes. Just as quickly as they arrived, they left.

"We ready to go?" Eko called from the bedroom.

He was oblivious to the chaos he'd just caused. I checked my watch. 7:30 am. Almost ten hours until we were due to be at the venue.

"Where are we going?" I asked, puzzled.

"Shopping. How much longer do you expect me to walk around in these rags?" He said.

He held up the last outfit we'd purchased for him the day before and looked at it in disgust. Almost instantly, Bug and I looked at each other and rolled our eyes. This newfound bonding moment caused us to fall over laughing.

"Something funny?" Eko hissed.

"Nope." Bug shot back.

His stern voice was all Eko needed to hear before retreating back into the master suite. Shortly after, we heard the shower start.

"I'll call the car service. Make sure he's downstairs in an hour." Bug said, rising from his seat.

With that, he was gone. Bonding session over.

Center City DC was a shrine to wealth. Over fifty high-end stores were nestled with two office buildings, a luxury hotel, and multiple condominiums. Eko had the driver pull up to the Hermes store first. A clerk was waiting at the front door with his usual champagne greeting.

"Is it empty?" Eko asked the store clerk as we approached.

"Yes, sir! The store has been cleared of all guests for your shopping needs." She said, holding the glass door open for us to enter.

Eko handed me an all-black MCM backpack and strolled in first.

"You're not coming?" I asked Bug.

He'd slipped on a pair of black shades and stood off to the side. He was once again back to business.

"No. I'll be out here. You go in with Eko. Stay close." He instructed.

My job description was continuing to grow longer and longer each day. I strolled in behind Eko and kept quiet as he picked up every fabric. After the third scarf, he looked back at me.

"Try this one."

He flung the scarf in my arms, and I moved the fabric between my fingertips. The red and white scarf felt like butter. Without hesitation, I quickly wrapped it around my neck. Walking over to the mirror just behind us, I checked myself from every angle.

"This is beautiful, but it wouldn't look good on you." I called back to Eko.

I didn't know much about high fashion, but I could tell that the scarf hanging around my neck was made for a woman. I could see Eko with his signature smirk standing behind me.

"It's not for me. It's for you." He laughed.

Feeling around, I found the price tag–$ 1,100.

"Oh, no!" I opposed it. Quickly unraveling the scarf from around my neck, I handed it back to him.

"Oh, yes." He retorted, pushing the scarf back into my hands.

The sales clerk watched our exchange in silence. She had just returned with a few women's blouses and pants. When she handed me the knitted pants, I stepped back.

"Look. You can't walk around with me in that."

I looked down at my all-black attire. This was a shopping trip. To me, shopping meant casual. I'd opted for black joggers and a black V-neck t-shirt.

"If you're going to travel with me, you have to dress…" He darted his eyes to the sky, searching for the right words.

"Better." The clerk chimed in.

I started to give them both my favorite finger but remembered that technically this was work. Stepping down from the small round pedestal in the store, I handed the scarf to Eko for a second time.

"Sorry that my clothes aren't up to your standards, but I can't afford any of this."

"You don't have to. Consider it one of the perks of the job. Everything is on me." He said.

The clerk returned to my side with two blouses and two pairs of pants. She'd added a few more scarfs and pointed to the fitting room behind me. I didn't object. This was a part of the gig. All I could hear was Windell's voice telling me to look the part. The inside of the fitting room was more superior than any department store I'd ever been in.

Each piece fit my body perfectly. The fabric seemed hand-stitched, and the material was made from nothing but the best. I tried on five outfits before Eko was satisfied, and we moved on to the men's section. Eko never looked at any tags or sizes. He would point, and the clerk would disappear to the back. Somehow, she would always return with the right size. Eko would feel each one's material, smell it, and then either shake his head yes or no.

"Do you buy wardrobes for all of your assistants?"

I'd taken my seat on the U-shaped couch and helped myself to a glass of the complimentary champagne. Though I'd only been doing this a week, I could already see I was getting used to the luxuries this life provided.

"Why do you do that?" Eko asked, ignoring my question altogether.

"Do what?"

For a second, I thought I had broken another one of his unwritten rules.

"Look down when you ask me questions. I noticed that you don't do that with anyone else."

For the first time, I realized that the voice and tone he was using changed. The obnoxious rich celebrity seemed to take a vacation. Even if this was short-lived, I was relieved.

"I was told you don't like being looked in the eye.

He laughed.

"I forgot she would give you all that rule."

It was the first time he'd brought up Addison since her untimely departure. He grew still after mentioning her name, which piqued my interest. I toyed with the empty champagne glass, looking for a way to ask without appearing nosey.

"How long did she work for you?" It was all I could muster up.

We were now walking towards shoes and handbags. So far, I didn't have to do anything but trail behind Eko from section to section. When he wanted something, the clerk would appear with notice–this part of the job I could get used to.

"She never really worked for me. Her father works for the record label. I met her when I first signed, and she'd been around ever since." He offered after a while.

"You miss her?" As soon as the words left my mouth, I knew I'd gotten too personal.

"You don't miss people in this business. People come, and people go. You learn to not get attached."

"You sound like an only child."

I knew the psych classes I took in college would come in handy one day. Who would have thought I would get to use them on an emotionally unavailable singer?

"Yup. Raised by my white mom and a Nigerian father."

"You're Nigerian?" I asked surprisingly.

Nothing in all the research I'd done labeled him as Nigerian. Or even bi-racial. He was marketed as a light skin black man who could sing.

"Yes. My name is Ekon. It means ``strong `` in Nigerian." He said in his native accent.

Hearing more about his background made his personality make a lot more sense to me. They say money really doesn't change you. It just enhances who you are. I was surprised at how candid he was being with me, given he'd just met me. I had so many more questions to ask, but our conversation was interrupted by three loud taps on the store window.

Bug was standing outside surrounded by a group of fans. I'm not sure how we hadn't heard the commotion before now, but fifty people were outside, with more coming up the street. They all screamed Eko's name when he looked up. Most already had their phones out in hopes of a picture.

"They always find me. Hand me that bag." He said with a grin.

Taking the backpack from me, he hands me a black AMEX.

"Finish up here and meet me in the car."

I stood at the counter and watched as Eko went out to meet his adoring fans. He hugged each one and took pictures with anyone who asked. I didn't even blink when the cashier said the total was over fifteen thousand dollars. I just handed the card over and took all six bags.

By the time I had gotten to the front door, Eko had handed out one hundred dollars bills to everyone. Before things could get too out of hand, Bug motioned for him to wrap it up. It was still another 15-minutes before we got in the car.

Riding back to the hotel, I couldn't help but think about all the horror stories shared the night before. Though I'd met the monster they described, today I got to meet the saint. I decided I would give him a little more grace. He can't be all that bad.

Chapter 10
"WE AIN'T SUPPOSED TO BE KISSIN'..."
– Marcus Graham, Boomerang

Capital One Arena was just a few short minutes from the hotel. Decked out in the new designer wear Eko had purchased earlier, I sat in the back of the sprinter looking over the show binder for the third time today. Bug helped me with anything I didn't understand while Eko slept. When we arrived at the venue, I was to go immediately to Eko's dressing room.

"Make sure everything on this list is in the room." He said, handing me a copy of Eko's rider.

The rider listed Eko's requests and would be different for every city. I wasn't expected to memorize it, but I was expected to make sure everything was in place each night. Tonight, Eko was feeling vegan. Everything in the room needed to be "vegan friendly." This included the materials the furniture was made of. I silently wondered how I was going to figure this out.

When I stepped into the room, I checked every box on the list twice. Every couch was made of vegan leather, and the tags were left on as proof. The food had been prepared by a vegan restaurant, and every ingredient was clearly labeled for Eko to see. I found humor in the fact that he'd just had bacon this morning. Once I'd signed off on the room, Eko was escorted in by Bug and venue security. After he was settled, I was to check every other dressing room for comfort. My first stop was the dancers' room. Since I had been promoted, the venue provided someone to do their steaming.

"You ladies need anything?" I asked.

"We're all set!" Lynne called from her place on the floor.

Each one of them was sitting with their legs crossed in the middle of the room. This venue gave them a space slightly smaller than the last, but they still managed to make it feel like the perfect piece of Zen. Candles were the only thing to illuminate the room, and the sounds of rain danced out of the surround sound speakers in the corner.

"You can stay if you want." Coco offered.

The peace I felt just from standing by the door made me want to take her up on that offer, but I still had one more stop to make. I smiled, and politely declined. Easing the door shut behind me, I made my way down the hall to Eight's room. His door was ajar, so I walked in.

Velvet curtains were fitted throughout an all-black room. The only light came from a small lamp in the corner. Eight leather recliner chairs sat in two rows of four in front of the plasma tv. I paced the empty room, making sure there were enough drinks and food. I felt every curtain along the way.

The last piece of fabric seemed oddly placed. Moving it to the side, I saw that it hid a full bar and every vice you could think of.

"Like what you see?"

Eight's voice shocked me, and I knocked over two bottles of champagne.

"I'm sorry!" I screeched.

I kneeled to the floor to start cleaning the glass, but Eight's hand on my shoulder stopped me.

"Don't worry about it. I have people for that."

I stood to my feet, but his hand remained on my shoulder. I glanced down but didn't ask him to move it. Eight studied my face for a bit before he squeezed behind me to the bar.

"Can I offer you a drink?"

I contemplated his offer. I wasn't sure if there was any rule against drinking on the job, but I figured one wouldn't hurt. I could have a drink and still make it backstage in time to catch the show.

"Sure." I spoke.

Eight turned his back and poured a little of this and that in a stemless wine glass. Handing me the drink, he took a seat in one of the recliner chairs. Without an invite, I took the recliner next to him and brought the glass to my lips.

"Ada."

Bugs voice made me sit straight up. He had a look in his eyes that made me feel like I had been caught doing something wrong. He looked past me to Eight and nodded. Unspoken words were had between the two, as I felt like I was caught in the middle of an awkward exchange.

I handed the drink I almost consumed back to Eight and walked towards Bug. I expected him to tell me that Eko needed something. Instead, he turned and started towards the stage. When we'd gotten halfway down the hall, he stopped and looked me square in the eyes.

"Let me give you a piece of advice."

He wasn't asking this time.

"When I said this wasn't a place to make friends. I meant it. Be. Careful."

His voice was stern as if chastising a child. I had no time to remind him that I wasn't one before he stomped away from me.

After watching the show in silence, Bug and I loaded the sprinter van while Eko was sound asleep inside.

"I'm sorry."

Bug's unexpected apology came as I handed him the last bag.

"For what?"

"How I spoke to you earlier. I just know how this business can be. You seem like a good person, and I would hate for this little world of ours to change that."

"Uh. Thanks. I guess."

The many sides of Bug were becoming confusing. One minute he was all business the next, he cared about me being a "good" person. I couldn't keep up. Nor did I want to. Climbing into the sprinter, I settled in the seat furthest to the back. Bug bypassed every available seat to sit next to me.

Ignoring his presence, I leaned in to the window and watched the unfamiliar D.C. streets float by. The slow-moving van lulled me to sleep after a while.

"Ada"

Bugs voice was soft in my ear. Somehow during the ride, my head decided to use his shoulder as a pillow. The van was now empty except for the two of us. I sat up in a rush.

"Everything is okay. Eko is already up in his room, and the bags were brought up by the hotel staff." Bug assured me.

Stepping down, he held out his hand to help me out. I accepted it, and we walked through the lobby at the same pace. Once inside the elevator, Bug punched in the code for our floor and stood opposite of me.

"You're like a sour patch kid." I blurted out.

"I don't get the reference." He said, staring straight ahead.

"One minute you're sour. The next, you're nice." I explained.

This made him laugh. I could tell he was contemplating if what I said was a compliment or insult. I honestly meant it as both. I figured this would be nicer than saying 'you're exhausting.' The elevator stopped before he could give me a response, and I didn't want to push him any further.

"Have a good night." I said once we both stepped off into the hallway. Eko's room was to the left, and his room was to the right. Here is where we separate.

"I think I'm more like a Tootsie Pop. Hard on the outside. Soft on the inside. You just never know how many licks it's going to take to get to the soft part." He said with a smirk.

When I got to the presidential suite, I searched for my room key. Still tired from the day, my purse looked like a puzzle in the dimly lit hallway. After checking three times, I knocked. There was no answer. Waiting a few moments, I thumped on the door again. Next, I heard soft music coming from inside.

Pressing my ear firmly against the door, I could hear the faint sounds of moaning mixed with the melodic sounds of Kem. I knew then my night was about to get longer. I stood in the hallway, pondering my next move before heading to the right.

I only had to knock on Bug's door once before he opened it. He didn't ask why I was there. He just stood to the side and let me in.

"I'm sure he'll be done soon." He said.

"How'd you know?" I said, plopping down on his couch.

"I've been doing this a long time." He chuckled.

Handing me a glass of water, he sat next to me and turned on the TV. His Netflix was already queued up for the next episode of Grey's Anatomy. I looked over at him in disbelief.

"Don't you say a word to anybody!" He quipped.

"Your secret is safe with me." I said, using my hand to imitate sealing my lips.

We watched quietly as one of the main characters, Derek Shepard, was hit by a semi-truck. As he was being rushed to the ER on the screen, I trembled. Without realizing it, I had slid closer to Bug on the couch as the doctors worked to revive him. When he was pronounced brain dead, I sobbed. Unsure of what to do, Bug paused the tv and turned to face me.

"You okay?"

"No. I'm not. It's just not fair!" I choked out.

"It's a character. He isn't dead in real life." He said, trying to console me.

"He is!" I protested.

Bugs' gaze was filled with confusion. He didn't know that an episode of Grey's would trigger me, and I felt it necessary to explain why. I told him all about Amare and his unfortunate passing. I even told him why I was no longer a nurse.

"I'm so sorry. If I'd known, we would have never watched this." He said, grabbing me into a hug.

He held me until my sobs subsided and then kissed my forehead, followed by the top of my nose. Feeling a sense of familiarity, I leaned in and softly kissed his lips. It was a short peck at first, but the second kiss was passionate. It started slow and steady. Then Bug took the lead.

Placing my face between his hands, he took his time with each kiss. Masterly dancing his tongue with mine, he leaned me back onto the couch. Two knocks on the door stopped us before we could get too far.

We stopped mid-kiss, not saying a word. Silently hoping that whoever was on the other end would go away. They didn't. Two more knocks came, and Bug stood to answer. On the other side was Eko.

"Finally! I found you." He said, looking relieved to see me sitting on the couch.

He briefly looked at Bug then back at me but never addressed the elephant in the room.

"Ada, I need you to call housekeeping for new sheets." That was all he said before heading back to his room.

Suddenly becoming embarrassed by my moment of vulnerability, I quickly hopped up and gathered my things. No other words were spoken between Bug and me. All I could hope was that he'd be all business again tomorrow.

Chapter 11

"YOU LIKE THEM THUGS, MAMA. THAT'S THE PROBLEM."
– Jody, Baby Boy

The next morning, I woke early after tossing and turning most of the night before. I wanted to avoid Bug for as long as I could. The thought of being confined on a tour bus with him for two hours to Philadelphia didn't help settle my nerves at all. I'd been in my personal cocoon for so long, I had forgotten what it was like to have physical interactions with someone. Hoping the hot water from a shower would wash the guilt from me, I stepped inside Eko's master suite while he slept silently.

When I arrived back to the room last night, I found myself feeling like I had cheated on Amare. I had gotten good at pretending like the life we once shared together was a fairy tale in a faraway land. Last night with Bug reminded me that it wasn't. More than anything, I needed to come to terms with the fact that I liked it.

I ran my fingers over my lips, remembering the soft kisses from Bug the night before. For a second, I could smell his cologne lingering inside the bathroom. Feelings that I hadn't felt for a while rose up. Eyeing the showerhead, I pulled it down to rest between my legs. Holding one hand on the wall, I propped my other leg up on the side of the shower. Tilting my head back, I allowed setting number three to remove any tension I'd been feeling.

The interruption of taps on the door ruined my fun before making it to the mountain top.

"Ada! Don't use up all of the hot water!"

Eko had a lousy way of inserting himself in everything. Last night he had been gracious enough to not say anything about why I was in Bugs room, nor did he mention how he knew to find me there first. We both waited in awkward silence for room service to replace the linen on his bed. Once they finished, he went to bed as nothing happened.

"I'll be out in a second!"

We stayed in a room that costs more than the average salary, and there was only one bathroom. I huffed loud enough to be heard outside and put the showerhead back in its rightful place. So much for tension relief. Finding a hotel robe, I threw it over myself and headed out towards the living room. Eko didn't waste any time barging into the bathroom behind me.

Slouching into one of the office's armchairs, I started fumbling through my bags for travel wear. The office in the suite was doubling as my dressing room. It was the most privacy I could find. Locating anything in the sea of black I packed was difficult. I made a mental note to ask Eko if this was a real rule or one of Addison's made up ones.

"You gonna get that?"

Eko was out of the shower and yelling from the other side of the office door. While changing, I hadn't heard the door, and of course, the superstar couldn't bother to answer it himself. Thankfully, I was fully dressed. When I arrived at the door, again I was surprised to find no one there. There was a small white envelope on the floor with my name on it.

Inside were twenty-five one-hundred-dollar bills. Unbeknownst to me, today was payday. When I'd gotten to the twenty-fifth hundred, I found a small white note tucked behind it. I recognized the small handwriting immediately.

Your secret is safe with me. – Bug

The bus ride to Philadelphia was quiet from the beginning. Bug hadn't spoken to me since we got on, only offering a few reassuring smiles. His note made this bus ride a lot less awkward. When he announced that he would take one of the bunks and nap, I opted to stay in the living room alone.

Flipping through the channels, I settled on old episodes of The Office. Even if it was only going to be for a few hours, I was learning to take my peace where I could find it. No Bug. No Eko. No dancers. I could finally just - Be.

"What you watchin'?

Eko poked his head from behind the bedroom door. I started thinking he was doing this on purpose or had a hard time being alone. I paused the episode.

"The Office." I mumbled.

"Oh, my favorite. Move over."

Eko pushed his way next to me on the couch. I darted my eyes from him to the empty couch across from us three times, hoping he would get the hint. He didn't.

"Why you lookin' like that? You high?" He asked.

"No." I said flatly. "I've never been high, and I don't plan to."

"You're missing out." He said, grabbing the remote and restarting the episode.

We watched Michael Scott's departing episode in silence. Annoyed that this had become a group effort rather than a solo mission, I kept my arms crossed. Eko didn't seem to notice or care. I'd seen this episode a million times. Michael finding unique ways to say good-bye to each character was heartwarming.

"I wish I could do that." Eko huffed.

"Care about somebody else besides yourself?" I said.

I didn't intend for my response to be so harsh but let's face it, I was right.

"No. I wish I could just up and leave everything behind."

Relaxing my arms, I leaned back into the couch. Eko had grabbed my attention.

"Leave the music industry?" I asked.

"If I could, I would leave all this shit behind." He said, staring at the ceiling.

"Where would you go?"

I was beginning to get the sense that my alone time would turn into a therapy session. I can now add this to my developing list of duties.

"I would start a non-profit and call it Keys to Success. It would be based in Nigeria. Teaching kids how to play the piano would be so dope. I'd build a studio, and they could come to make music for free."

The celebrity ego had been shed. Eko had a boyish grin the whole time he described this ultimate dream. He explained his plan with such enthusiasm. Even going so far as to tell me how much everything would cost. He'd made the amount to start it three times over at this point. He continued to ramble on and on.

"You can do it." I encouraged him. "Why not just let this be the last tour you do? Take some time and go follow your dreams."

The light in his eyes started to dim. My voice had brought him to the here and now.

"There are such things called contracts. It's not that easy."

His revelation silenced me. In my world, his ideas were easy to accomplish. He had the money, the means, and even notoriety. My instinct was to find a solution. I went through all the ways he could get out of whatever contract he was in. I even toyed with how he could be an international star from Nigeria.

I was so caught up trying to fix a problem that I didn't notice Eko had fallen asleep until my shoulder slumped down. Not one to wake someone from sleeping, I grabbed the throw blanket from behind me and draped it over his body.

I waited a few minutes to make sure he was fully asleep before turning the tv back on. Being an assistant to Eko was like having a child. You rest when they rest. With the commercials becoming white noise, I leaned my head back and drifted off.

My leg shook violently, and I sat up to see Bug sitting across from me. He looked from me to Eko and then back to me. I couldn't read his facial expression before he got up. His body language told me he wasn't pleased with what he saw. The sour was back.

"We're here." He said before walking off the bus.

Shrugging my shoulder, I woke Eko. Our hotel for the night was The Ritz Carlton in downtown Philadelphia. An all-white building with pillars like The White House. The hotel took up almost the entire city block. We stepped off the bus to a beautiful sunny day.

Bug was waiting. Remembering my duties, I headed first to the lobby. Bug called my name to stop me.

"We don't have time for check-in. We must head to the video shoot. The driver will be here in 5 minutes." He said once I'd turned around.

I hadn't had a chance to read the notes for today's events and was surprised to hear that we had another engagement besides the concert. I didn't question him, and within five minutes, we were inside the sprinter van headed towards a public housing division in south Philadelphia. As we rode, Eko threw a notebook in my lap. I opened it and found lyrics written on the first page.

"I need you to read these to me, so I can memorize them before the video shoot. I can't look like I don't know the words." He said, pulling out a tray table to roll up more weed.

The child-like man I'd encountered inside the tour bus was gone. He'd quickly been replaced with the arrogant, nonchalant performer. His personality changed almost as fast as Bugs. I suppose that is why they got along so well.

"Didn't you write these?" I asked as I began reading through the lyrics silently.

"Writing your own shit is for old washed up motherfuckers. I'm hot, young, and rich. Being rich means you pay broke motherfuckers to write it for you." He said with a smirk.

Bug shot a look at him that said he'd heard this speech one time too many. I was hoping I would never listen to it again. When I stumbled over every lyric, Eko didn't seem to be bothered by it.

He'd just look at me with amusement and have me reread it. The song he was featured on was for an up and coming rapper from Philly simply named BM. Eko was determined to not look foolish in front of his peers. We went over his short part ten times in the thirty-minute ride.

When we pulled up to the Philadelphia Housing Division, every street was blocked off. The driver pulled onto a side street, and the video director arrived to escort Eko to the set. When I stood to follow, Eko waved me off

"What are we supposed to do?" I asked Bug.

"Sit here and wait for the shoot to be over. Being seen with security and an assistant is bad for his image out here."

I didn't dare ask why. I took my seat in front of Bug and wished I'd brought a book to pass the time. The quietness was uncomfortable. I shifted a few times and tried my best not to look back at Bug.

"Can I ask you a question?"

I shook my head, no. I had a feeling he wanted to have a conversation about last night, and I wasn't prepared for that just yet.

"It's not about last night." He said, reading my mind.

"Then, sure." I said.

"Why are you doing this? Even without nursing, I'm sure there's something more you can be doing."

I shrugged. I wasn't prepared for this question either.

"There must be something else you'd rather be doing." He probed.

I let the statement linger for a while. The last time I opened up to Bug, we ended with a kiss. I felt like I needed to keep my guard up with him. We'd crossed a line last night, and I needed to try my best not to cross it again. On the other hand, it had been so long since someone asked me what I wanted to do. The attention was refreshing.

"Bug – " I started.

"Call me Brenden."

"Brenden, I would rather be running my own clinic." I said, still too afraid to look at him.

"Why don't you?"

"I have one hundred thousand reasons why."

"Ah, money."

"Yes, money. It costs at least one hundred thousand dollars to start a clinic. That doesn't even include what it would take to keep it running.

When he didn't speak, I turned to read his face. To my surprise, his expression looked like mine when I was trying to find a solution for someone. I anxiously awaited his response that never came. The rattling of the sprinter van window startled us both.

Bug slid the door open to find the video director flushed red. He was panting as if he'd run miles to get to us.

"It's Eko! He passed out in the middle of the street!"

Chapter 12

"I WANT TO MAKE LOVE TO YOU TONIGHT.

– Jordan Armstrong, The Best Man

My adrenaline took over before Bug had a chance to respond. Hopping out of the van, I asked the director to show me where he was. We ran two blocks to where a crowd had begun to form. In the middle, Eko was lying on his back, shaking uncontrollably. The streets had now changed into my ER.

I instructed everyone to clear the way. Leaning down, I took Eko's pulse. The pulse was slow but present. Next, I turned him on his side. Moving in closer, I began to monitor his breathing. While taking my time to listen to his body, I noticed the absence of sirens.

"Did no one call the ambulance?" I called out.

Everyone stared at me as if I'd spoken in a different language. Bug had just managed to get to the scene. I motioned for him to come over. By now, the shaking had subsided, and I was ready to put Eko on his back.

"He's had a seizure. Help me get him on his back." I directed.

With a count of three, we slowly rolled Eko over. Though he had stopped shaking, his breathing hadn't gone back to normal, and he was still unconscious.

"Does he have a history of seizures?" I asked Bug

He looked as if he was contemplating telling me the truth. We had no time to beat around the bush.

"I can't help him if you don't tell me." I called out

"Sometimes, he drinks lean. It's cough syrup mixed with soda and candy."

"I know what lean is." I rolled my eyes. "Where is the ambulance?"

"They didn't call one. Eko is a celebrity. We don't want the press. This has happened before; he always comes to." He finally offered.

"Well, it's been five minutes, and he still hasn't come to." I mocked. "You either call the ambulance, or I will."

There was no time to play nice. Though I no longer belonged to the medical community, it was my duty to not let someone die if I could help it. Bug pulled his phone from his pocket and dialed 9-1-1. Within minutes an ambulance showed up and lifted Eko onto a gurney. I chose to ride in the ambulance with Eko while Bug followed us in the sprinter.

Without thinking, I grabbed his hand and squeezed it. At this moment, I was no longer his assistant. He had become my patient. The ambulance sped through the streets, but Eko still hadn't opened his eyes. The EMTs placed an oxygen mask on his face and began to take his vitals.

Pretty soon, I could feel Eko's hand squeezing mine. I looked down to see his face filled with panic. He fought with the EMT but eventually lifted his oxygen mask.

"Ada... am I going to die?" he squeaked before passing out again.

Bug and I had been waiting in a private section of Mercy Medical Center for hours. Eko's celebrity status brought him through a secret entrance on the side of the hospital. Peeking up at Bug, I could see the anguish on his face.

After giving my update to the nurse on call, I was escorted by two nurses to this small private area where Bug was waiting. We hadn't spoken a word since. I tried to find words to comfort him, but every time I started, nothing seemed right. Rescuing us from the soundless room was a petite brown skin woman. I assumed she was a nurse and hopped up to meet her.

"Do we have an update?" I eagerly asked.

"Marie." Bug called from behind me.

Marie stepped past me and brought Bug into a warm embrace. They stayed that way for what seemed like an eternity before releasing each other. Suddenly I was the odd man out. Detecting my puzzlement, Bug stepped in the middle of us.

"This is Marie. She's Eko's publicist."

I stretched my hand, and she accepted. I could tell she had no idea who I was, and she looked to Bug for confirmation.

"This is Ada. She's taken Addison's place."

Nodding her approval, she took a seat in the small metal chairs and motioned us over.

"We're going to cancel the Philly show. I was able to spin this and have the press release state that he passed out from exhaustion. We have two shows scheduled in NYC, but I'm unsure if that is going to happen."

She handed me her card and told me to update her as soon as we knew more about Eko's state. She'd flown in from New York to check on Eko and take care of any loose ends at the venue. As quickly as she came, she left. Returning Bug and me to the hush of the empty room.

"I should have been with him!" Bug banged the table with his right hand.

It was the first I'd seen him react to everything that happened during the day. Magazines went flying as he let out a choked scream. Lowering his head, he walked towards me. I stood to receive him. Falling into my arms, he let out a soft cry into my shoulders.

I did my best to stay upright under his weight. Everything he had been holding in, he was letting out right here. I squeezed him, rocked him, and whispered it would be okay. I said that in his ear over and over. At this moment, the hospital disappeared. It was only the two of us. Single footsteps brought us back to reality.

"I have an update for Ekon." A voice from behind us called out.

We turned to see a doctor holding a chart. He struggled with the pronunciation of Eko's government name for a bit before we both told him to just say Eko.

"Uh, yes. Eko. He's stable. We've given him plenty of fluids, but he will need to stay overnight. The seizure has taken a lot out of him, and we don't believe he's completely out of the woods yet."

"Can we see him?" Bug asked.

"Tomorrow. Right now, we think some rest would be best."

Realizing there wasn't much more we could do here. We thanked the doctor for his care and left the hospital. While waiting for our car to arrive, I texted Marie a short update. The sprinter pulled up just as I'd hit send.

Moving to the back, we sat next to each other. So close that our shoulders overlapped, and our thighs touched. It's incredible how anguish and grief can bond two people. Though I prayed Eko would recover fully, I knew all too well what it felt like to think that he wouldn't. I intertwined my hand in his to bring comfort. We let the silence continue on the ride back.

Sans Eko, there was no red carpet rolled out for us when we arrived. Marie had handled the check-in process and arranged for everything to be brought up to the presidential suite. Bug grabbed our keys while I waited in front of the elevator. Not having to rush allowed me to take in the lobby, which was dome-shaped and entirely fitted with marble.

"Have you eaten?" Bug asked, interrupting my gawking.

The day had grown long. Eating hadn't even crossed my mind. Hours in a hospital will do that to you. Worry overshadowed all other needs that day.

"No, I haven't." I said, stepping onto the elevator.

"How about dinner in my room?" He offered.

"Dinner?" I questioned.

"Yes, dinner. It usually happens in the evening. There will be food and even drinks involved."

I was happy to see his sense of humor return. The person who had just poured everything out seemed to be coming back to life. Not wanting him to be alone, I accepted his dinner offer.

"I'll just need to go shower and change first." I said as we stepped off the elevator.

"Cool. I'll see you soon."

With that, we went our separate ways. I'd gotten two steps down the hall before it dawned on me.

"Bug." I called out.

"Yeah?"

"Your secret is safe with me too."

Showering a little longer. Getting dressed a little longer. Pacing a little longer. All things I did inside the presidential suite before I got the nerve to head back to Bugs room. When I got to his hotel room door, I paced again. The door eased open without me having to knock.

"I thought I heard something. What are you doing out here?"

"I was just about to knock." I lied.

His eyes stayed on my face for a bit before letting me in. The room had been dimly lit. Guiding me to the dining room, he handed me one of his signature drinks.

"I didn't know what you would like, so I ordered a little bit of everything."

Ten plates of food were spread out on the table. Each labeled with its own card. Portions of pasta, chicken, steak, and seafood were plated elegantly with their own side dishes. I glanced back at Bug, who I could tell was looking for my approval.

He'd changed out of the clothes he wore earlier and was now in black jeans and a plain black t-shirt. I had opted to wear one of the designer skirts and silk tops Eko purchased for me. Suddenly, I was feeling too overdressed.

"You look nice." Bug offered with a smirk

"Thank you. Everything looks good."

I reached for an empty plate to fill, and Bug stopped me. Grabbing an empty plate in each hand, he served both with food. After I was satisfied with the small food samples on my plate, he carried them to the living room. Instead of our usual Grey's Anatomy, he turned on light classical music as a backdrop.

I hid my surprise at his tastes in music. There was no need for a heated exchange. Instead, I picked at my food. Everything I tasted was heavenly. The steak melted in my mouth, the seafood was perfectly cooked, and the pasta tasted as if it was homemade.

My mouth was filled before I noticed that Bug had gone silent. He hadn't touched a bite of his meal.

"Normally, when you invite people to dinner, you eat with them." I said playfully, nudging his shoulder.

"I'm sorry. I'm still worried about my friend. He's passed out before, but nothing like this."

His voice was barely a whisper. I pushed my plate back and moved closer to him on the couch. Facing me, I could see his eyes begin to well with tears. Giving him a reassuring smile, I kissed his forehead, followed by his cheek. We stared at each other before he leaned in to kiss my lips.

This time I didn't feel any guilt, only longing. Our tongues danced passionately before Bug abruptly stopped. Thinking that we'd gone too far, I slid back. Bug stood. Pushing the table a few inches, he dropped to his knees in front of me. His eye told me we were about to go further.

Grabbing my waist, he slid my panties down with one hand. My skirt was now sitting above my waist. His gaze asked me for permission to go forward. I parted my lips and said yes. Taking two fingers, he parted my second set of lips, massaging back and forth until I cried out.

Soon, he replaced his fingers with his tongue. Small short kisses between my thighs started the fire. His tongue dipping in and out, kept it going. Tilting my head back in pleasure, I gripped the edges of the couch. Taking my thighs and placing them on his shoulders, Bug lifted me. Palming my ass, he continued his sweet torture as he carried me to the bedroom.

My moans could be heard through the city. Only when I reached my personal finish line did he release me to the bed. Catching my breath, I watched as he undressed. He was naked within seconds. Turning his attention to me, he tugged at my skirt and threw it to the floor. I made quick work of my shirt before he could even reach for it.

This wasn't a drill. This was happening. Grabbing me by the waist, Bug pulled me to the middle of the bed. He lay on top of me and started kissing my neck. The feel of my human weighted blanket made me moan. His kisses soon led down to my breasts. Sucking each one before stopping once again.

Leaning over me, he opened the drawer on the nightstand and pulled out a condom. Standing on his knees, I watched as he rolled the latex from the tip to the base. I spread my legs and arched my back to receive him. He went slow, easing in an inch at a time. Resuming his position on top of me, he slowly continued to enter. When he'd filled me up completely, I winced.

"You okay?" He moaned in my ear.

"Yeah. You're just bigger than I thought." I said, adjusting my body underneath him.

He took my statement as a challenge. Placing my right leg over his left shoulder, he started a slow and steady rhythm. I picked up on it almost immediately, and we moved in unison. In and out, up and down. Our movements were slow and steady at first. Then we threw away all ease and moved with fury.

Just when I thought I had enough, he found a way to flip me on my stomach. Placing all his weight on mine, we went back to slow and steady. The pace seemed to represent both of our personalities. Before long, I had found my place at the finish line once again. This time I called his name loud.

My body's trembling seemed to affect him, as he soon forcibly shook on top of me. Rolling off me to the other side of the bed, he quickly pulled me into his embrace. I lay in the middle of his chest and once again searched for my breath.

"I GOT A SHOW TO DO, BABY."
– James 'Thunder' Early, DreamGirls

"Ada, come take a shower with me."

I didn't move.

"Come on!" Bug said while stripping the covers and slapping my ass.

"We don't have much time."

I heard him walk towards the bathroom, and then the steam from the shower soon filled the room. The encore performance was getting ready to begin. The shower had a long marble bench that wrapped around inside it. When I dragged myself into the bathroom, he was already seated. He looked at me through the glass and patted his thighs.

Stepping into the hot water, I accepted his invitation. I sat, allowing him to fill me up once again. Sucking his bottom lip, I slowly rocked my hips back and forth. When our rhythm got really good, he flipped it. Standing up and taking me with him.

With my thighs on his forearms, he gave me slow and easy strokes. Locking eyes with me, he smirked. Knowing that I was about to lose control, he moved even slower. In and out. In and out. I focused on keeping up with him until I heard small faint taps. We paid no attention to them at first, trying our best to finish what we'd started. Then the taps became bangs, and Bug stopped.

"Urgh!" He breathed into my shoulder.

He never released me, though. Still, inside me, he pressed the button to stop the shower.

"Bug! Open Up!"

Eko. Now it was my turn to sigh. We stared at each other for a few seconds, wondering if we had heard what we thought.

Bang. Bang.

"Don't make me go to the front desk and get a key!"

If we didn't know, we knew now. Somehow Eko had made it from Mercy Hospital back to this hotel. Bug eased me down to the floor of the shower. Putting one finger to his lips, he grabbed a robe and headed to the front door. I tiptoed out of the shower. Holding a towel to cover me, I sat on the edge of the clawfoot tub. I could hear them talking.

"You saw Ada?" Eko hissed.

"Nope. I ain't seen her. I just woke up. How did you get here?" Bug lied so quickly, I believed him sitting two feet away.

"Damn. Do you think Ada quit? Andie already left last night; we can't afford to lose anymore." His voice sounded full of panic. I contemplated revealing myself to ease the worry but thought better of it.

"Uh. I'll go look for her. I'm sure she didn't quit."

"Wait! You got a groupie in here?!" I heard Eko sniff the air as if he could smell sex from the hallway.

I put my head in my palm. More silence before Bug spoke.

"Yeah! I got a groupie in here. You had me stressed. I needed to have a little release." He faked a laugh.

"Well, carry on! I'll call her again."

I heard the loud clap of a dap and then the door closing.

"Ada." Bug called. "It's safe."

I came out of the bathroom to find Bug already finding clothes to wear for the day.

"How is he out of the hospital?" I asked, looking for my skirt.

"I don't know, but you should get down there."

Bugs all business persona was back. He handed me my shirt, and I pulled it over my head in silence. Holding my flats in my hand, I moved from the bedroom to the front door. Bug followed slowly behind. Before I could turn the knob to exit, he grabbed me back into his embrace. He cupped my chin and leaned in. Three kisses followed.

Forehead. Cheek. Lips.

While I slid down the hallway, my phone buzzed in my hand. When I finally looked at it, I had ten missed calls and just as many text messages from Eko. The phone started to ring again. I lowered my tone and answered on the fourth ring.

"Hello."

"Where are you?" Eko yelled

"I went for coffee." I said, lying for the second time in the last twenty-four hours.

"Well, bring me some."

I wasn't expecting him to ask for coffee. In the short time we'd been together, he never asked for coffee. Champagne, yes. Whiskey, sure. Never coffee. Pausing to think of my third lie, I faked a sigh.

"I wanted decaf, and they didn't have any. So, I came back."

"That's alright. Just get here as quickly as you can."

Standing in front of the presidential suite, I eased on my flats and pushed the door open. To my relief, I could hear the shower running in the master suite. I eased into the Livingroom and quickly changed from my dinner attire to leggings and a long-sleeved shirt. Making my way back to the bedroom, I tapped twice on the bathroom door.

"I'm back. I'll be in the Living Room when you're done." I said.

"Come in!" Eko called from the other side of the door.

Placing one hand over my eyes, I eased the bathroom door open. On the floor in front of the tub sat Eko. He didn't look like he'd just gotten out of the hospital. He'd already changed into black knit pants and a matching top.

"What are you doing here?"

"I checked myself out this morning. I can't afford to miss 100k!" He said, trying to pick himself up.

His body began shaking from the sudden movement, and he quickly fell back to the ground.

"You should be at the hospital," I said, rushing to his side.

"I need you to wash my hair." He said, ignoring my question.

Seeing that nothing was going to get him back in a hospital bed, I stood in search of hotel shampoo. Leaning his head back over the side of the tub, I began to work the shampoo into his hair. I tried my best to not get too close, for fear he'd smell the scent of Bug and sex oozing through my pores. Just in case he had, I asked a question to distract him.

"What did you mean by you can't afford to miss 100k?"

"I get paid 50k a show. I have two shows at the Barclay Center in New York. Fifty plus fifty equals one hundred." He said, amused with his corny joke.

Rinsing his hair, I grabbed for the towel to the right of me. I wrapped his hair with it and sat him up. Drying it and standing in front of the mirror, he seemed to be satisfied.

"Be honest. You left because the lights are off in hospital rooms." I said, trying to make a joke of my own.

He grunted while staring at his reflection in the mirror.

"I ain't afraid of the dark if that's what you think. I grew up poor. Our lights always got cut off. I promised myself when I got a little money, I'd never be in the dark again."

His speech left me dumbfounded. My ill-placed joke hadn't gone over as I thought. Eko seemed to just let it roll off his shoulders.

"I need you to get everyone on the bus within the hour." He said, walking out the door.

"Okay. I just need one thing." I said back.

"What?" He shot back.

"A shower."

Later that morning, we began our journey to New York. As the bus rode along, Eko marched from the front to the back of the bus. Andie had left the show as soon as she heard of Eko's hospital stay. Assuming that there would be no tour, she took another job. Eko learned this news from Marie just before checking himself out of the hospital.

I had spent the first hour of the ride calling every dance studio in New York to find a replacement. Every time we'd thought we found someone, Eko found something wrong with her. Too tall. Too short. Too small. Too Big. I had grown tired.

"What if you just use three dancers?" Bug asked.

We hadn't spoken one word about last night. He went back to business, and I went back to being the assistant. Every so often, I would catch him staring at me. We'd exchange smirks and then go back to ignoring each other. Every bump the bus hit activated the soreness between my thighs and reminded me of just how close we were the night before.

"Ada. How much you weigh?"

Eko had stopped his pacing and was eyeing me suspiciously from the corner.

"I don't know. 135."

I looked over to Bug for an explanation, but all he could offer was an "I don't know" shrug. Eko disappeared to the back of the bus and returned with a laptop.

"Watch these." He said, sitting next to me and queuing up YouTube.

"Why would I need to watch your old videos?" I questioned.

"Because you're going to dance with me in place of Andie tomorrow."

I started to object, but Eko had already started his way back to his bedroom. Searching for rescue in Bug, I looked over at him. He, too, had nothing to offer me before heading back to his bunk. Hitting the PLAY button on the video, I couldn't help but think of all the things that could go wrong with this.

I spent the night rewatching the videos—each time, I was reminded of how bad an idea having me perform was.

"What have I gotten myself into?" I whispered to the silent bus.

Chapter 19

"I KNOW YOU DON'T SMOKE WEED. I KNOW THIS, BUT I'M GONNA GET YOU HIGH TODAY!"
– *Smokey, Friday*

Five. Six. Five. Six. Seven. Eight

Eko and I had been in the conference room of The Baccarat Hotel in downtown Manhattan for over three hours. I was no closer to getting the four steps he'd taught me.

"Ada! This ain't hard! Coco! Show her again!" Eko was beyond frustrated with me.

I stood to the side and let Coco take center stage. Standing in front of Eko, she took three slow and steady steps toward him. When they were nose to nose, Coco slid her body down his. She quickly spread her legs and looked back at the audience of chairs seductively. Reaching down, Eko lifted her and dipped her into his arms.

Staring at her, he began to mouth the words to his song. When he got to the last line of the verse, he planted a soft kiss on her lips and brought her upright. Standing straight up, she glided away, occasionally looking back at Eko with a flirty stare.

"That's it. Then you run off stage and let us take care of the rest." Coco called from the corner.

Just like that, she was back to her bubbly personality. The sexy, playful dancer was gone.

"Let's go." Eko instructed.

I stood in the same place as Coco and started again. This time I pictured that Eko was Bug. Being intentional with every step, I walked closer to him. Sliding my body down his, I tried to keep my balance while using my hands to slowly spread my legs. Just like he'd done with Coco, he raised me up and dipped me into his arms.

Just before he could kiss me, I moved away.

"That's what I'm talking about! This is how you dance tonight!" He yelled, clapping his hand excitedly.

Seeming to not notice my resistance to put my lips on his, he picked me up and spun me around.

"Just remember to lean into the kiss next time."

With that, he was out the door, leaving me to continue practice with Coco. Lean into the kiss, I thought. What could go wrong with that?

That night at The Barclays Center, we all gathered in Eko's dressing room. When we arrived, he handed each of us a glass of champagne. I had managed to fit into the form-fitting leotard and made sure to not move too much. The last thing I needed was for the material to rip. Standing in the circle, I couldn't keep my hands from shaking. I tried to focus on my breathing, but I could barely see when Eko stood to speak.

"We have thirty minutes until showtime. I don't have to tell y'all how important this show is." He started

At the sound of thirty minutes, my stomach started to do flips. I rubbed it a little before finding a seat near the door.

"Over nineteen thousand people are waiting for us. Let's give them a good ass show!" He yelled.

Everyone cheered and held their glasses high. I wanted to join in on the celebration, but instead, I doubled over. Without notice, everything I had eaten that day was on the floor. Nothing kills a party better than throwing up.

"Everybody out!" Eko called

When I tried to stand. Eko stopped me.

"You stay." He said.

Once everyone had gone, the maintenance crew came to clean up my mess. I apologized more times than I could count before heading to Eko's private bathroom to clean up. When I returned, Eko had rolled a blunt and was holding it between his fingers.

"Sit." He pulled out a chair, and I sat down.

"I'm sorry - " I started to apologize again, but he waved me off.

"What you need to do is relax." He said, taking a lighter to the blunt.

Taking two puffs, he handed it over to me. I declined.

"Two puffs aren't going to make you a heroin addict, Ada." He pushed the blunt into my hands.

Visions of me throwing up on the stage scared me enough to try it. Mimicking what Eko had just done, I placed the blunt between my lips. Inhaling slowly, I felt the smoke fill my lungs. Once I had gotten the hang of it, I took another pull. Then came the coughing.

"That's enough." Eko called.

Taking the blunt from me, Eko stood.

"See you on stage." He said.

The effects of the blunt didn't take long to settle in. Walking out of the dressing room, I immediately felt lighter. I giggled at nothing and everything.

"What's so funny?"

Bug was standing right outside of the door. I had passed him without even noticing.

"Nothing." I said, suddenly feeling embarrassed about my impaired state.

"Are you doing okay? They told me about your little incident."

The word "incident" made me laugh out loud. Bug quickly grabbed my chin between his thumb and index finger. Tilting my face up, he moved in close. Expecting a kiss, I leaned in. He stopped me and stared into my eyes for longer than usual.

"Are you high?" He hissed.

"Yes." I giggled again.

"Ada" He sounded disappointed. "Don't let him pull you in."

"I won't. He's not." I couldn't find the words when everything seemed to float around me.

"I care about you. Don't make me regret that."

He disappeared again. Sour Bug had come out to play tonight. I wanted to follow him, but

I was grabbed by Lynne. The lights were just about to go down, and I needed to take my place. I could only hope I'd get a chance to explain myself later.

I rocked side to side behind the curtain, waiting for my time. The weed had mellowed me out, and I let the energy from the crowd energize me. The chants were deafening. Eko started his show as he always had. When the piano stopped, I knew it was my time to go. I didn't have time to second guess myself.

Remembering all that Coco had taught me, I strutted towards Eko. I didn't miss a step, and neither did he. When Eko dipped me into his arms, there was a pause. Taking the mic with his free hand, he sang a few lines of the song. Just as we had rehearsed, at the last line, he leaned in to kiss me. This time I didn't move, and he pressed his lips against mine. Counting to ten in my head, I was prepared to be lifted and walk off stage.

That didn't happen. Eko held the kiss longer than I'd expected, and in the essence of playing along, I didn't reject. Eventually, he lifted me, and I strutted off the stage like I was told. Feeling a different type of high, I beamed with excitement once I got out of everyone's view. My joy was short-lived because in the shadows stood Bug. His expression let me know that he didn't share my excitement.

Thinking about how the kiss must've looked from his angle, I started towards him to explain. I didn't get two steps in before he turned to walk away.

After the show, we were the last to leave the venue. Eko was obligated to appear at a club not too far away. In the van, I made sure to sit right next to Bug. He stared at me but didn't say a word. Eko sat in front of us, oblivious to anything going on. Feeling bold, I leaned in and kissed his cheek. Next, I placed my hand on his thigh, hoping it would ease some of the tension between us. It didn't. As quickly as I put it, he removed it. Realizing we weren't going to call a truce tonight, I moved to the seat furthest away.

The line to the club was wrapped around the corner. Eko's name shined big on the sign above the front entrance. Not one to miss an opportunity to be seen, Eko made sure the driver let us out right in front. Once inside, we were escorted to a VIP section on the top floor. The dancers, Eight, and a few unfamiliar faces were waiting for us. Eko started us off with shots of dark liquor. Trying to ignore the death stare Bug was giving me, I took three back to back.

Eko grew tired of our small section and invited us all to the dance floor. Taking two more shots, I followed behind. No one else decided to accept his invitation. Bug reluctantly followed us both. It didn't take Eko any time to find a redhead to dance with. Starting a slow step, I moved closer to Bug.

He was standing still in a sea of dancing bodies. Grabbing his hand, I spun myself around. Arching my back, I moved my hips in a circle to the slow reggae beat. Before long, I felt him pull me closer. We started a slow grind.

Bug continued to groove with me through three songs until I suddenly felt him stop. A commotion across the floor grabbed his attention. Realizing Eko had started to argue with a tall, muscular gentleman in the corner, he headed that way. The redhead looked like she was trying to diffuse the situation. The liquor flowing through my system allowed me to not care. Staying where I was, I danced alone.

From where I stood, I watched Bug take care of the issue. After talking to the redhead and her friend, he escorted Eko back to the VIP section. We locked eyes, and he motioned for me to join them. I shook my head. Though the dance floor was shoulder to shoulder, I felt by myself. Between the weed and shots, I couldn't feel anyone's presence but my own. Watching the DJ on the stage, I moved to my own concert for one. Before long, I could see Eight walking towards me.

He was holding two drinks, and when he got close enough, he handed me one.

"Hey. Eko told me to bring this down." He yelled over the music.

The music was so loud that he had to press his lips to my ear for me to hear. I took the glass from him and sipped. I couldn't place the type of liquor inside the glass, so I took another gulp. Eight was watching me closely. Stepping in, he put his lips on my ear again. Whatever he said was soundless.

Somehow the music has gotten extremely loud, and I asked him to repeat himself. When he stepped in for a second time, the glass he'd given me fell from my hands. I watched Eight's lips move to ask me if I was okay.

Suddenly the room became foggy. The walls felt as if they were closing in on me. My head, which was clear just a few minutes earlier, was now fuzzy. Frantically I looked around for Bug or Eko. My eyes only saw blurred lines. Offering me his hand, I followed Eight outside to the night air.

Once my foot hit the pavement, I threw up. Still not being able to make out much, Eight looked at me with concern in his eyes. He began talking, but I couldn't make out a word he said. Realizing that I wouldn't understand, he pointed to a black sprinter van that looked like one I had ridden in earlier.

I shook my head quickly. Yes, I needed to sit down. Hopefully, whatever was taking over my body would subside. My legs felt like bricks, and I couldn't imagine what I looked like to the people I passed. Eight kept my hand tightly wound in his until we reached the van. Sliding the door open, he placed me inside. His mouth moved to say something else, but I had lost all hearing at this point.

Sitting in the seat, I knew that this was something more than alcohol or weed could do. Panic setting in, I tried to sit up but couldn't. My body was slowly starting to shut down. I watched in fear as Eight stepped into the van and sat next to me. Before he could close the door, I felt a hand from outside, grab me just as everything around me went completely black.

Blinking twice, I adjusted my vision to the star lights on the ceiling of the sprinter van. In the distance, I could hear Bug and Eko speaking in a low whisper.

"Nah! He has to go!" Eko whispered.

I sat up and coughed.

Alerted to my presence, Bug raced to my side.

"Ada! Do you know where you are?"

I felt hungover. My mouth was dry, and my head was spinning. Sitting up proved to be a struggle, so I laid back flat on the seat.

Reaching up, Bug grabbed a small bottle of water. Placing my head in the small of his hand, he leaned me up to take a sip. The cool water seemed to help me come back to life.

"Yes, I think so." I replied.

Eko looked over the seat at my face with concern. After I'd finished the small bottle of water, his eyes softened. Seemingly satisfied with my state, he turned and grabbed his phone. When the person on the other end answered, he turned his back to us.

"Eight is fired!" He hissed into the phone.

He didn't give the other person a chance to answer before he pressed end. Confused, I sat upright just as we were entering the hotel's front entrance.

"It wasn't Eight's fault. I shouldn't have had that last drink you sent me."

I couldn't bear the thought of someone getting fired over my irresponsibility. Eight had been nothing but gracious from what my memory could recall.

"I didn't send you a drink." Eko said.

Bug and Eko shot looks at each other. Neither speaking to me directly.

"What is it?"

Had I blacked out and done something crazy. I panicked. Would I be on TMZ the next day?

"Eight drugged you." Bug finally revealed.

"No. Eight didn't. Eight wouldn't." I was shocked and all over the place.

"Yes. Eight did, and Eight would." He said.

"How would you even know that? The club was dark, and you were nowhere near us."

"I saw him drop a small white pill in your glass. I called for you. I ran after you."

He trailed off. How could I have not noticed? I searched my memory for clues but came up short. Sliding the van door open, he stepped down and reached for my hand. Using him for balance, I entered the cool night's air. Taking one step, I shook.

One foot over the other, I stumbled forward. Only to be saved by Bug's arms. Picking me up, he carried me through the lobby. I felt like I was floating in his arms. I could only imagine what the hotel staff must be thinking. I hid my identity in Bug's shoulder.

Making it to Eko's room without getting noticed, Bug placed me on the couch in the living room and headed towards the door.

"Watch her." He instructed Eko, who'd just walked in behind us.

"Where are you going?" I asked from the couch.

"I forgot something at the venue. I'll be back."

He was gone in a flash. Eko looked at me like I was a sick puppy he didn't know what to do with.

"You can take the bed tonight. I'll take the couch." He offered.

My insides were tightening, and I couldn't put the words together to tell him yes.

"You heard me? I'm giving you the bed." He repeated.

I opened my mouth to thank him, but the only thing that came out was the contents of my stomach.

Chapter 15

"THIS IS A SNAG OF TREMENDOUS PROPORTION."
– Smokey, Friday

When I had finished emptying my stomach on myself and the couch, I looked to Eko for help. Without hesitation, he hoisted me onto his back and ran to the bathroom. On my knees in front of the porcelain God, I was emptying out whatever was left. Eko was standing behind me, holding my hair. Occasionally he would slap cold water onto my face.

"How much more could you have in you?" Eko spat.

Choking on my own vomit was not the way I saw this night's ending. When I felt like I had nothing left, I pushed Eko to the side and lay on the cold marble.

"You can't stay like that." Eko said, look down at me with disgust.

He held his nose closed to the smell that was rising off my soiled shirt. Putting myself in the fetal position, I turned away from him. I could feel him staring for a while before he disappeared out of the room. Rocking myself gently, I said a silent prayer. This world had done what I said it wouldn't. Suck me in.

I thought of the red flags that had been thrown at me that night. I had let my guard too far down. Being too friendly put me in danger. Bugs warnings echoed in my ear as I prayed again for nausea to end.

"Here." Eko was back.

Turning to face him, I could see he was holding a pile of clothes. He placed them gently on the floor next to me.

"I went through your bag. I hope you don't mind. You need to take a shower. Do you need help getting up?"

I raised my hand and waved no. Eko didn't listen. Stooping down, he grabbed one of my arms and stood me straight up. Placing both hands on my shoulders, he stared into my eyes.

"You good?" He said.

Embarrassment kept me silent, but I nodded my head, yes. Starting the shower, he placed his hand under the water to test its temperature. Once it was to his liking, he stood up and walked towards the door.

"I'm going to wait outside the door. Just in case you pass out again."

I scrubbed my skin until it was sore. Standing under the hot water, I turned the gauge to make it even more scalding. I needed to wash off every memory from tonight. Though nothing had happened, I thought of all that could have. That made me gag again. Spitting out water on the shower floor, I screamed then caught my breath.

If I could have, I would have stayed under the water all night. Not wanting to alarm my newfound caregiver, I decided against it. I ended my cleansing and stepped out. Eko had brought me a t-shirt and shorts. After I got dressed, I helped myself to a hotel robe before walking out into the bedroom.

Eko was sitting with both legs crossed in front of him.

"I thought I was going to have to come in there." He said

I gave him a thumbs up. He nervously checked his phone.

"You still haven't heard from Bug?" I asked, sitting on the edge of the bed.

"Nah. I texted a few times. He hasn't responded."

I was sure I had something to do with him, not responding. I was not exactly his favorite person right now, and though he pitied me, I know that he had his own feelings about the situation. If he wanted space for the night, he deserved that.

"Thank you for saving me tonight." I said to Eko as I sat on the edge of the bed.

"Don't thank me. That was all Brenden. He never took his eyes off you. He tried to stop Eight, but the club was just too packed. I'm just glad he could make it to the van before things got really crazy."

"You still fired him for me." I countered.

"I fired him for everybody. I can't have that liability around." He said.

He was being nonchalant, but I knew deep down he cared. Hearing Eko piece together, the gaps of my memory didn't make me feel any better. It only made me want to put this night behind me faster.

All of a sudden, exhaustion hit me like a ton of bricks. I lay back on the pillowtop bed and covered myself in blankets. Closing my eyes, I welcomed the sandman. Feeling the opposite side of the bed move from a new body entering it, I popped my eyes open. Eko had sat on the edge of the bed and was preparing to lay down.

"You said you would take the couch." I whined.

"You threw up on it, remember?"

Laying, so his feet rested by my head and his head by my foot, he turned his back towards me. He was fully clothed; I know that was for my benefit. With no energy to fight, I hurried the furthest I could move away from him and resumed my journey to dreamland.

"Don't worry. I won't bite you." Eko called out as I was drifting off.

That night my dreams were carefree. Bug and I were walking down a street I had never seen. Hand in hand, we strutted down the pavement to a destination unknown. When we arrived at an interaction, we both stopped. I looked into his eyes and began to speak, but nothing came out. Holding my face between his two hands, he just stared.

The staring only stopped when we heard a loud crash behind us. The colliding of metal shook me awake. When I opened my eyes, Bug was still staring. This stare was not one of love or admiration. Instead, it was one of irritation.

Bug smelled like a fresh shower. He was dressed in a t-shirt and jeans. I briefly noticed that his face was slightly swollen on one side. I reached up to touch him, but he swatted my hand away.

Anxious, I looked to the empty space where Eko had been last night. In his place lay only a robe. Waking completely, I could hear the shower running. A trail of his clothes was leading to the bathroom. Even I knew this looked bad. Bug looked sickened by me as he left the bedroom.

"Wait!" I called behind him. "Let me explain."

Slumping his shoulders, he kept right on

"This isn't what it looks like. I threw up!"

Not understanding what that had to do with him finding me in Eko's bed, he reached for the door. Making one last effort, I forced to pass him and blocked his way.

"Please let me explain." I repeated.

"You don't owe me anything. All the groupies make it to the bed. You just took a little longer than I thought. Shit, at least I got to sample some too."

His words cut like daggers. I started to explain again, but he gently pushed me out of his path. His cold eyes stared at me one more time before slamming the door so hard it shook. Motionless, I contemplated running after him. Hearing the word groupie play in my mind caused me to stay.

Turning around, I saw Eko standing in the entryway to the living room. I wondered how long he'd been standing there. Not wanting to have this awkward conversation, I dropped my head.

"Don't worry. Brenden will get over it." Eko snickered.

"How do you know?" I said.

"He has a little thing for you. It started the first night he met you in Magic City. Brenden never likes anyone, and he likes you. Believe me, he will get over it."

I appreciated Eko trying to reassure me, but it didn't help. My intuition told me that it would take more than time or space for this to be resolved.

Chapter 16

"YOU GONNA LET THESE MEN MAKE YOU GO CRAZY, WHILE THEY GO ABOUT THEIR LIFE WITHOUT A CARE IN THE WORLD."
– Tasha Mack, The Game

Eko continued his routine as nothing had happened. His friend being in pain only seemed to bother me. After showering and changing, he rushed me to do the same. I felt much better after my shower. Whatever toxins had entered my body the night before seemed to be gone now.

"You don't have to perform tonight."

Eko gave me permission that I wasn't going to ask for. My dancing career was going to be one night only. I felt like that was one night too many. As I called performers to replace Eight, my thoughts continued to stay on Bug. We still hadn't heard one word from him. The space he needed, I would give him until after the show. Rather than let things fester, I decided to face him head-on.

Everyone jumped at the chance to work with Eko. He didn't care who I chose, just as long as the spot was filled. Once I'd made the final selection, it was time for us to head downstairs to the second show. When we passed Bug's room, I stopped and tapped twice. When he didn't answer, I started to drum on the door again.

Eko grabbed my arm to stop me.

"He will meet us in the car. Let's go." He said.

After waiting in the van till the final minute, Eko leaned up to the driver.

"Leave him." He instructed.

I was torn between the job I signed up for and the loyalty I had created with Bug. My heart ached, knowing I may have hurt him. Slumping back into my seat, I rode back to the Barclays Center in silence. When we arrived, the streets were flooded with fans. They were all eager to see Eko in his final show in New York.

At the back entrance, we were greeted by a tall, older white gentleman. He seemed to be at least ten years older than us, with a head full of white hair. Dressed in a grey suit and wing-tipped shoes, he stepped forward to greet Eko.

"My name is Stanley. I'll be protecting you this evening."

Eko looked at me. I could offer him no explanation. Suddenly my phone buzzed in my back pocket. Excited to see Bug's contact information flash across my phone. I immediately opened the text.

Stanley will be helping with security for tonight. Show him the ropes. If you have any questions, text, Marie.

His text was just as cold as he had been earlier. I read the text to Eko. Only then did he shake Stanley's hand and proceed backstage. Not seeming to be phased, Eko went on as usual. Later that evening, I watched the show in a daze. It was difficult being backstage without Bug's presence. I went back to his text, searching for clues that weren't there. I continued to go through the motions, becoming more and more nervous as we neared the show's end.

While I went through my regular routine of packing Eko's bag, I went over my speech to Bug in my head repeatedly. When Eko finished his performance, I was waiting patiently in the van. As we rode through the traffic, I watched the blocks pass by. We'd been here for two days, and I never paid attention to the bright lights. The lights served as a distraction for what was about to come next.

When we arrived at the hotel, I left downstairs Eko with Stanley. I refused to sit any longer with my thoughts. Standing in front of Bug's door, I banged twice. I used my fist to make sure he heard me. After the fifth time, he still had not answered. I cursed under my breath. Stepping off the elevator with Stanley standing close behind, Eko looked at me suspiciously. I wondered how desperate I must've looked.

I waited for him to investigate further, but he strolled down the hall without a word. Sitting on the floor in front of the door, I decided to stay. When he didn't open up after a few minutes, I decided to give my speech anyway.

"Bug – I mean Brenden." I started to stutter almost immediately. Even though I had practiced this a hundred times in my head, the words were lost on me now. I tried my best to piece them together, anyway.

"Whether or not you decide to talk to me again, I need to say my piece. I would never do anything to purposely hurt you. I know what you saw. I know what it looked like. I just need you to know that it wasn't that. Somehow, I care about you. I hope I don't regret that."

Feeling defeated, I stood to my feet. In the distance, I heard the presidential suite door open. Eko poked his head out the door. When he saw me still sitting there, he chuckled. I wondered how much of my one-sided conversation did he hear.

"He's not there." He called.

"Where is he?" I said, walking closer to him.

"Bug is on a plane back home to LA." He held his phone towards me.

Taking it from his hand, I started to read the text on the screen.

> Concert life isn't for me. Headed back home. You're in good hands with Stanley. I'll check in soon.

The text mentioned nothing about me. Suddenly, I remembered Eko's words. "People come, and people go. Don't get attached." Apparently, Bug followed those same rules. Letting me in, I walked to the living room to find a new couch. Folded neatly were two throw blankets with two pillows on top. Eko left me with my typical sleeping arrangements. Setting up the pillows first, I reached to unfold the throw blanket. A small note fell from inside.

Take care of yourself - Bug

I woke up before dawn the next day. Packing in silence, I woke Eko just before seven am. Our next city would be the longest. We had a nine-hour drive to Detroit ahead of us. I reread Bug's note before placing it with the others inside my bag.

There were no lines to read in-between here. Bug said what he meant to say. Though a familiar sadness had settled inside me. I pushed it to the side. I had broken the cardinal rule. Somewhere I had stopped focusing on making money. Instead, I had made a friend. Maybe even a lover.

Not knowing if what I felt for Bug was real, I was reluctant to even acknowledge it. I lied to myself and said it was just a fling. Nothing more. Boarding the bus, I planned to ride to Detroit quiet.

Stanley would be flying to Detroit, leaving Eko and me to ride alone. Once on the bus, Eko went straight to his room in the back. I'm sure my sorrow was evident. It seemed to fill the space Eko's quick retreat let me know he wanted no parts of it. I was relieved to be left in the living room alone. I slid a pair of headphones over my ears and hoped the music would ease my pain.

It wasn't until Eko's door burst open that I realized the music was too low.

"Turn on the news!"

Marie's voice was screaming through the speakerphone. I searched for the remote and turned on the television. Breaking news flashed across the screen.

Up and coming rapper assaulted outside of the hotel. No potential suspects.

The news anchor was standing outside of the hotel we had just left. Eight was found lying in a small alleyway behind the hotel. The hotel stated that their security cameras malfunctioned, and there was no surveillance footage. A broken jaw, black eye, and broken ribs were just a few of his injuries. His assistant had found him only after he'd stopped answering her calls.

I watched the story in horror, thinking to myself, who would do this? Deep down, I already knew the answer. Not wanting to say it out loud, I covered my mouth in disbelief. Eko didn't seem to be phased. Once the breaking story had left the screen. He sighed and ended his call with Marie.

"Whoever did it should have killed him." He said before heading back to his room.

Chapter 17

"YOU ARE A PERFECT VERSE OVER A TIGHT BEAT."
– Dre Ellis, Brown Sugar

We entered Detroit in the early evening. Our next show wasn't scheduled until the following night. Eko must've really felt bad for me because he made sure to get a two-bedroom suite. The first chance I got, I retreated to the second bedroom. Eko poked his head in once I was under the covers.

"You want dinner?" He asked.

"Nope." I said, hoping to end all conversation.

"There's a spa downstairs. Feel free to treat yourself." He offered.

"I'm good." I said.

Catching the hint, Eko left me alone. At this point, I was just...there.

Periodically I would check the news for updates on Eight. I wasn't really concerned with how Eight was doing. I wanted to know if they had any suspects. So far, the report was that Eight would recover completely. The police continued to interview him, but he refused to give any information. There was only one person I knew who was capable and had a motive.

I pushed that thought out of my mind. Now I started to worry about Bug for all new reasons. Wanting to at least know that he was okay, I sent a text.

> Got your note. Just wanted to know that you're okay. I miss you.

I deleted the last line before hitting send. My blue bubble appeared. Shortly after, three grey bubbles floated across the screen. Anticipating a response, I sat straight up in the bed. The grey dots disappeared, and no message followed. At least I knew Bug was alive. It'd only been a day, but I craved him still.

I felt like a complete fool. After all, Bug had only been a small part of my life. If I could survive the death of my husband, this shouldn't be bothering me as much.

"Tighten up!" I yelled to the ceiling.

Kicking my feet up, I started music therapy. Searching through playlists on my phone, I settled for classical music to remind me of simpler times. The soft music gave me the calm I was looking for. Relaxing, I started to doze off. Before sleep could fully wrap me in its arms, Eko burst through my room door.

"Get up. I need you to go somewhere with me." He demanded.

I gazed at him from my bed but didn't move. I hoped my body language told him I wasn't going anywhere. Grabbing the corners of the blankets, he tossed them to the floor.

"Get up!" He repeated.

"Why? Where are we going?" I said, still not getting up from the bed.

"We're going to get your man back." He said with an eye roll. He sounded like a character on a corny sitcom.

Even with his antics, I didn't ask anything further. Rising from the bed, I dressed quickly. Not sure where we were going, I trusted he had a plan.

Eko had arranged for a car to take us to Royal Air Charter in Detroit. When we arrived at the tarmac, there was a private plane waiting for us. On the ride over, Eko was very tight-lipped on his plans. Telling me to just let him work. Having dealt with his craziness for so long, I figured there couldn't be anything much worse he could do.

Stepping out of the car, we were greeted by our pilot and stewardess. The small plane was made to fit nine people comfortably. Having never flown private before, I was once again in awe. Cream-colored furniture lined the entire aircraft. You could see wood accents throughout. Two leather chairs faced each other on my right, while a full couch sat on my left. There was plenty of extra seating in the back.

"Champagne?"

The stewardess offered us two glasses as soon as we sat down. Eko happily took a drink. I politely declined and asked for water instead. My prior experience with alcohol left me with a bad taste in my mouth.

"This is your captain Greyson. We will be flying non-stop from Detroit to Los Angeles. Please sit back, relax, and enjoy the ride.

The captain made the announcement just before instructing the stewardess to prepare for take-off.

"LA?" I asked Eko.

"Yeah, I found out that Bug is working a job for Jane Blade."

"Who is Jane Blade?"

"She's a new female rapper. She stays pretty local. Not many people know her. "

It made sense. Bug wanted to be on a smaller stage. He'd chosen someone who would really be able to let him hide in plain sight.

"What's the plan?"

"The plan. I don't really have one. All I know is, when we get there, you don't talk."

"I don't talk?"

"No. You've gotten us into enough trouble already. Let me take the lead. I will get this all straightened out. "

Eko seemed to be content with himself. Even though he was delusional, at least he was consistent. I was only along for the ride. If it meant clearing the air with Bug, I was all for it. The four and a half hour flight seemed to rush by in a blink of an eye.

Once we'd landed, Eko let me in on the fact that Bug would be at a small concert venue called The Regent. Another car was waiting for us as soon as we touched down. Once inside, we headed to Downtown LA.

The show had started by the time we arrived, and there was no one outside. Taking the lead

Eko went to the front door and walked right in. The security guard didn't question either of us. When asked where the backstage entrance was, he offered to show us. From behind, I could spot Bug standing towards the opening of the stage.

Eko called Bug's name loud down the hall. When he turned around, I could tell from his face that he was surprised to see us. I knew then that Eko had left out the part that Bug didn't know either of us were coming.

Meeting us in the hallway, Bug looked over at me then to Eko.

"What are y'all doing here?" He asked Eko.

Eko got straight to the point.

"If this was anyone else, I would say fuck it. Since it's you, I'm going to make it right. Nothing happened between us. We slept in the same bed, and that was it." He said.

I could tell by his tone that Eko was over the mini soap opera we had him starring in. Bug didn't answer right away. He looked at Eko suspiciously and then me with disdain.

"You put him up to this?" He asked.

"You know me better than that." Eko said, answering for me.

Bug still didn't take his eyes off of us. People passed us with curious expressions while Bug was trying to decide what to believe. He let more time go by before grabbing Eko into a hug.

"We're good, man." He said once they'd separated.

Stepping around Eko, he stood in front of me next. I remained where I was. Before long, he grabbed me into a hug too.

"We're good too, Ada."

I melted in his arms and let out a deep sigh. It felt good to have so much pressure relieved.

"I wish I would have known; this was all you needed." I said, still holding on to him.

"Eko left a show. That was all the confirmation I needed." He chuckled.

"I never got a chance to thank you for saving me." I said once he released me from his embrace.

"You don't have to thank me. When I love someone, I go hard for them."

"You love me?" I questioned.

"Yes. I do. Don't make me regret it." He said with a smirk.

Jumping into his arms, I wrapped my legs around his waist. If I was being honest, I loved him too. I'd found love in the most unusual place. A love that I never thought I would find again. Who knows what would come of us, or if we'd even make it. Even so, I was willing to try.

Eko clapped his hands twice, and we both looked his way.

"This is cute. I'm happy for y'all. I really am, but we have a plane catch." Eko was butting in once again.

"Come with us." I said, smiling at Bug.

"I can't right now. As soon as the show is over, I will meet you in Detroit." He said, kissing my lips.

He took a few minutes before unwrapping me from his arms. Not wanting to leave his embrace, I lingered too. Realizing that neither of us would move, Eko grabbed my arm and dragged me back towards the front entrance.

"See you in Detroit!" I called Bug.

Eko fell asleep as soon as we took off back to Detroit. I was still beaming when I finally joined him. The dream of Amare and I on our first date replayed. Everything happened the same as it always had. When I returned to the restaurant, instead of it being empty, Amare was now waiting. I went to speak, but no words came out. He smiled at me and handed me a note.

Don't be afraid to move on. I'll always be with you.

Chapter 18

"THERE'S A THIN LINE BETWEEN LOVE AND HATE."
– Ma Wright, A Thin Line Between Love and Hate

The Fillmore in Detroit was no different than any other venue we had been in during the tour. Just like the other stops, fans filled the building. Yet, I had an eerie feeling as we pulled to the back entrance. Just before we left the hotel, the news reported that Eight checked himself out of the hospital.

Eko didn't seem to be worried or anxious. Everyone else around us was. Before we stepped out of the sprinter van to enter the location, Stanley went over the security concerns with us again.

"We have intel that someone in Detroit may want to hurt you. We are in Eight's hometown. Your name hasn't been associated with his unfortunate accident publicly, but people believe otherwise. I know that he isn't too happy with how you handled things. I'll ask again, do you want me to bring in extra security tonight?" He said.

Eko scrunched his face up. Stanley had given this same speech in the hotel room and then again when we left. I felt like we should tell Stanley about my episode with Eight but kept quiet. Eko and I never talked about Bug being involved. Though we didn't know for sure, I think we both had an idea.

"You asked again, so I'll repeat it. No." Eko spat.

Before we left the hotel, he'd spoken the same words. His mind was on completing the last show on the first part of his tour. After the performance, he could take some much needed time off. I was concerned about his well-being, but my mind was trying to find the words to tell him that I wouldn't be returning for the next six dates.

Stanley looked troubled but didn't say anything more to Eko. He escorted us into the dressing room and took his place right outside of the door.

"Call everybody in here. I have an announcement to make." Eko demanded.

I collected everyone, and we gathered in Eko's dressing room. Standing in a circle, we all waited to see what announcement he would give. Before he could say anything, our attention turned to the door.

A short bald man dressed in khakis and an oversized sweater entered and stood next to Eko. He sat a black briefcase on the table in front of us. I got the immediate feeling that something was wrong. Holding a glass of champagne, Eko stood on a coffee table to get our attention.

"I know y'all have been working hard. I also know that I'm not the easiest person to work for or with. This being our last show for a while, I wanted to show a little appreciation. "He said.

The bald man opened his briefcase and took out a stack of black envelopes. He began passing them out to each person. The envelopes were thin, and each one of our names were printed on the front. Once everyone received their envelope, we all joined hands. Coco led us in prayer.

"Lord, let us be protected, let us be in sync, and let these people experience the best damn show they've ever seen."

"Amen!" We said in unison.

When everyone piled out of the room, I thought this would be the best time to let Eko know I wouldn't be returning after this show. Wringing my hands, I waited for him to change in the restroom. As soon as he came out, I stood from my place on the couch.

"Eko, I have something to tell you." I started

"Well, it's going to have to wait." He said.

Looking behind me, I could see Stanley impatiently waiting.

"Eko, we need to get you to stage," Stanley spoke.

I would have to give my resignation another time. Following behind, Eko turned to me.

"Stay back and open your envelope first." He said with a grin.

Leaving me alone in the room, I toyed with the envelope in my hand. Opening it, I found a check for $1,000,000 made out to me. Attached was a small note.

Start your clinic. Just don't name it after me. One of us should be able to follow our dream.

Standing backstage, I was still speechless at Eko's generous gift. I don't know when Bug shared my aspirations with him, but I was grateful he did. Walking toward the stage entrance, I could hear Eko's piano solo ending. From a distance, I could see Coco standing behind the curtain, ready to do the routine she'd done so many nights before. Suddenly a dark-haired woman dressed in uniform pushed past me.

Her hat sat low on her face, and she kept her head down. The dark-haired woman walked right past Coco as if she was invisible. The back of her shirt read "SECURITY." Stanley must've ignored Eko's request for no extra security.

"Excuse me." She said to Coco.

It was her voice that gave her away. She'd lost some weight, changed her hair color, and was dressed commonly. But she couldn't change her voice. It was still high-pitched and squeaky like the first day I had met her at the dance studio. Picking up my pace, I tried to get to the stage and ask what she was doing here.

I was seconds too late. Just as Coco was entering the stage, she pushed her hard. Falling over, she looked back at me, stunned. I ran past the curtains to the stage but was pushed down by Stanley. Addison had made it to Eko before either of us.

She reached in her pocket and pulled out a small handgun. Holding it steady, she let off two shots in point-blank range before Stanley tackled her to the ground. I lept up with a vengeance. Finding Eko lying on the ground, I assessed his wounds. I could hear him gasping for air.

"Hang in there!" I said, trying to comfort him.

Seeing the blood pool around his chest, I screamed for help. Security lifted his body, and we met the ambulance at the back door. Eko's eyes were darting frantically, but he didn't speak a word.

"It's going to be okay." I said, holding his hand.

The ambulance sped through the Detroit streets, not stopping until we reached The Detroit

Medical Center. The doctors rushed to pull Eko from the back of the ambulance and provide medical attention. They instructed me to wait in the private waiting area on the 5th floor. Riding the elevator up, I said a prayer of my own. Standing in the empty waiting area, I was grateful that Eko's celebrity afforded me a place to cry without onlookers. Folding myself in a small metal chair in the corner, I rocked slowly. My lips trembling, I cried out.

The time seemed to stand still as I waited for an update on Eko's condition. Just as I was about to take matters into my own hands, A blonde woman in a white coat approached me.

"Are you Ada?" She asked.

"I was told to update you on Eko. He has just gotten out of surgery. The bullet barely missed his heart. We were able to remove the bullet, but his vitals aren't good. We will need to see if he makes it through the night." She said, flipping pages on his chart.

"Can I see him?" I asked.

"Yes, but you'll need to make it quick." She said, walking towards the patient rooms.

I felt a sense of déjà vu as I walked to his room. If it hadn't been for the number of tubes running through his body, I would have thought he was sleeping peacefully. I sat beside his bed and grabbed his hand. I squeezed it, but he didn't squeeze back.

"Eko. I don't know if you can hear me but thank you. You got on my last nerve for most of the time we were together, but you've shown me a lot. Thank you for the check. For funding my dreams. Also, try not to die. Please." I said, squeezing his hand again.

I knew too well what it was like to not say your last words to someone. I didn't know if these would be my last to Eko, but I couldn't take the chance. After squeezing his hand a few more times, I headed towards the door. The smell of the room, the beeping of the machines, all of it was triggering.

When I stepped out into the hallway, I put my hands on my knees and breathed deep. My body was starting to shake from the inside out. Once I felt I was stable enough, I stood up. A tall figure was staring at me from a distance.

"Is he alive?" Bug asked when he got close enough to me.

"Barely." I whispered

"You okay?" He said, caressing my face.

It was his turn to be the strong one now. Taking two steps in his direction, I let my body collapse into his arms.

Chapter 19

"CHEERS TO LOVE, HAPPINESS, AND ALL THAT OTHER SHIT"
- *The Brothers*

Ada! You got flowers."

Lauren had popped into my office, holding a bouquet of white roses.

"Is there a card?" I asked, looking up from a chart.

"There isn't a card, but it did come with a letter."

She handed me a black envelope with my name printed on the front. Recognizing who it came from, I opened it immediately.

"Thank you, Lauren." I said distractedly.

Noticing a change in my posture, she made sure to leave quickly. Inside were three pieces of paper folded neatly. I held the white pieces of paper in my hand. Sitting, I unfolded them and started to read the neat handwriting.

Dear Ada,

First, congratulations on the first anniversary of your clinic. I keep up with everything online now. Who would have thought we would both be living our dreams!? Keys to Success is going well, it took some time to get it started, but the kids love it! I'm trying my best to get used to my new life in Nigeria.

I don't get all the same perks over here, but they have fine dining and nice fabric. I hope you like the flowers. Give Bug my love. Let him know I'm rooting for him during medical school. The check enclosed is for the baby. Thank you for inviting me to the shower, but I think I should stay put. Congrats.

With Love, Eko

I instinctively rubbed my growing belly. Feels like just yesterday we were wondering if Eko would live or not.

It took some time, but Eko recovered from his gunshot wounds. The second half of the tour was canceled, and he spent months in recovery. Bug and I helped him every step of the way. When he was fully healed, he could buy himself out of the contract with his record label.

After shooting Eko, Addison fled the scene. She was found at a nearby hotel. It took thirty-six hours, but the police eventually talked her out. Once in custody, she sang like a canary. The gun she used had been given to her by Eight.

Using her emotions against her, he'd talked her into impersonating security to get backstage. The court process took months, but Eko showed up at every court date. He even testified. In the end, both Addison and Eight were found guilty of attempted murder. The day after the convictions,

Bug and I drove Eko to the airport. Staring death in the face caused him to reevaluate what was important.

Speaking of Bug and me, we decided to settle in Atlanta. We'd purchased a home in the suburbs to be closer to my brother. Jane Blade was the last security job Bug ever did. After we found out that Eko would need physical therapy, we all pitched in to help him recover. When Eko was ready to be back on his own, Bug removed himself as security and enrolled in the Morehouse School of Medicine.Bug removed himself as security and enrolled in the Morehouse School of Medicine.

We were able to take the money Eko had given me to pay for his education and start my very own clinic. The Amare Wilson Clinic for the underserved opened on the westside of Atlanta. My first order of business was to hire Lauren. She jumped at the opportunity to move to Atlanta from Chicago.

We had done more in a few years than most couples do in a lifetime. I still enjoyed our pace just fine. To this day, I never asked Bug about the incident with Eight. Though I had my own ideas, I felt some things were better left unsaid. When he wasn't in class, Bug interned at the clinic.

We got engaged shortly after the clinic opened. Just six short months ago, we found out that there would be an addition to our family.I was finally starting to find my groove again. Interrupting my trip down memory lane was a few faint knocks on the glass outside my door.

"Are you ready to go, Ada?"

Bug had stepped into my office dressed in his blue scrubs.

"Yup." I said, tucking the note back into its envelope.

I decided I would tell Bug about our gift from Eko later. He grabbed my bags and then extended his hand to help me up.

The name Bug had gone away. We only called him Brenden at the hospital. Occasionally at home, I would call him by the name I first met him under, and he would laugh. The best part about us is that sometimes I would still receive little notes from him when I least expected it. Bug has taught me that all love is unexpected. Whenever we receive it, we must take note of it.

CPSIA information can be obtained
at www.ICGtesting.com
Printed in the USA
LVHW010928190121
676761LV00007B/141